THE
EENTSY, WEENTSY SPIDER

FINGERPLAYS AND ACTION RHYMES

COMPILED BY
JOANNA COLE
AND
STEPHANIE CALMENSON

ILLUSTRATED BY
ALAN TIEGREEN

A Mulberry Paperback Book   New York

TO JOSHUA AND ZACHARY DANNETT

For their help in researching this book, thanks to Celia Holm, Children's Librarian at the Donnell Library in New York City, and to Mrs. "Mike" Vuillemenot and her staff at the Cyrenius H. Booth Library Children's Room in Newtown, Connecticut.

Printed in the United States of America.
First Mulberry edition, 1991
10
Library of Congress Cataloging-in-Publication Data
Cole, Joanna.
The eentsy, weentsy spider : fingerplays and action rhymes/
compiled by Joanna Cole and Stephanie Calmenson; illustrated by
Alan Tiegreen.
p.   cm.
Includes index.
Summary: A collection of play rhymes intended to be accompanied by
finger play and other physical activities.
1. Finger play—Juvenile literature.   2. Rhyming games—Juvenile
literature.   [1. Finger play.]   I. Calmenson, Stephanie.
II. Tiegreen, Alan, ill.   III. Title.
GV1218.F5C62   1991
793.4—dc20   90-44594   CIP   AC
ISBN 0-688-10805-9 (paper)

CONTENTS

FINGERPLAYS AND ACTION RHYMES

Fingerplays and action rhymes, like nursery rhymes, have been kept alive for generations because children love them. The musical language of the rhymes makes them easy to say and remember. The actions, too, are perfect for children, who love to participate. It's fun to make the tickly little steps of "The Eentsy, Weentsy Spider" climbing up the waterspout, to pretend to pound in a nail while singing "The Hammer Song," and to tip over your whole body for "I'm a Little Teapot."

Many of the rhymes reflect a child's world. They are about mealtime and bedtime and families. They are about the natural phenomena a child sees every day—rain, flowers, animals large and small. And they give children an opportunity to learn about left and right, up and down, and their bodies from head to toe.

So say them, sing them—there are musical arrangements at the back of the book—act them out. They really are fun!

TEN LITTLE FIREFIGHTERS

Ten little firefighters
Sleeping in a row.

Ding, ding goes the bell,

And down the pole they go.

Off on the engine, oh, oh, oh.   Using the big hose, so, so, so.

When all the fire's out, home so slow.   Back into bed, all in a row.

BALLOONS

This is the way
We blow our balloon.

Blow!

Blow!

Blow!

This is the way
We break our balloon.

Oh, oh, no!

TWO FAT SAUSAGES

Two fat sausages

Sizzling in the pan.

Pop!

One went POP!

The other went BAM!

 # SIX LITTLE DUCKS

Six little ducks
That I once knew.

WIGGLE FINGERS

Fat ducks, skinny ducks,
Fair ducks, too.

But the one little duck
With a feather on his back,

He led the others with
A quack, quack, quack.

Down to the river
They would go,
Wibble-wobble, wibble-wobble,
To and fro.

But the one little duck
With a feather on his back,

He led the others with a quack, quack, quack!
Quack, quack, quack. Quack, quack, quack.
He led the others with a quack, quack, quack!

OPEN, SHUT THEM

Open,
Shut them.

Open,
Shut them.

Give a little clap.

Open,
Shut them.

Open,
Shut them.

Place them in your lap.

Creep them, creep them.
Creep them, creep them

Right up to your chin.
Open wide your little mouth,

But do not let them in.

RAIN

Drum fingers on floor

Pitter-pat, pitter-pat,
The rain goes on for hours.
And though it keeps me in the house,

It's very   good for   flowers.

APPLES

Way up high in the apple tree,

Two little apples smiled at me.

shake arms

I shook that tree as hard as I could.

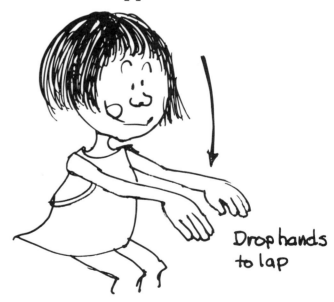

Drop hands to lap

Down came the apples—
Mmm, were they good!

TEN LITTLE FINGERS

I have ten little fingers,
And they all belong to me.
I can make them do things.
Would you like to see?

I can shut them up tight

Or open them wide.

I can put them together

Or make them all hide.

I can make them jump high

Or make them go low.

I can fold them up quietly
And sit just so.

THE QUIET MOUSE

Once there lived a quiet mouse In a quiet little house.
When all was quiet as can be,

OUT POPPED HE!

GRANDMA'S SPECTACLES

Here are Grandma's spectacles,

And here is Grandma's hat;

And here's the way she folds her hands
And puts them in her lap.

— 19 —

I'M A LITTLE TEAPOT

I'm a little teapot,
Short and stout.

Here is my handle.

Here is my spout.

When I get all steamed up,
Hear me shout,
"Tip me over and pour me out!"

🍵 HERE'S A CUP 🍵

Here's a cup,

And here's a cup,

And here's a pot of tea.

Pour a cup,

And pour a cup,

And have a drink with me.

BLUEBIRDS

Two little bluebirds
Sitting on a hill,

One named Jack,

The other named Jill.

Fly away, Jack.

Fly away, Jill.

Come back, Jack.

Come back, Jill.

GREAT BIG BALL

A great big ball,

A middle-sized ball,

A little ball I see.

Let's count them all together—
One,

Two,

Three!

MY HAT

My hat it has three corners,

Three corners has my hat.

If it did not have three corners,

It would not be my hat.

THE EENTSY, WEENTSY SPIDER

ARMS GO UP
AS FINGERS
"CLIMB"

The eentsy, weentsy spider
Climbed up the waterspout.

Down came the rain

And washed the spider out.

Out came the sun

And dried up all the rain.

And the eentsy, weentsy spider
Climbed up the spout again.

UP TO THE CEILING

Up to the ceiling,

Down to the floor.

Left to the window,

Right to the door.

This is my right hand—
Raise it up high.

This is my left hand—
Reach for the sky.

Twirl hands

Right hand, left hand,
Twirl them around.

Left hand, right hand,
Pound, pound, pound.

 # HERE IS THE CHURCH

Here is the church.

Here is the steeple.

Open the doors

And see all the people.

HERE ARE MOTHER'S KNIVES AND FORKS

Here are Mother's knives and forks.

Here is Grandma's table.

Here is Sister's looking glass.

Rock cradle

And here is Baby's cradle.

THE HAMMER SONG

Jenny works with one hammer,
One hammer, one hammer.
Jenny works with one hammer.
Then she works with two.

Jenny works with two hammers,
Two hammers, two hammers.
Jenny works with two hammers.
Then she works with three.

Jenny works with three hammers,
Three hammers, three hammers.
Jenny works with three hammers.
Then she works with four.

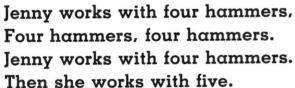

Jenny works with four hammers,
Four hammers, four hammers.
Jenny works with four hammers.
Then she works with five.

Jenny works with five hammers,
Five hammers, five hammers.
Jenny works with five hammers . . .

Then she goes to sleep!

 **MY TURTLE**

This is my turtle.
He lives in a shell.
He likes his home very well.

He pokes his head out
When he wants to eat.

And he pulls it back
When he wants to sleep.

 # FIVE LITTLE KITTENS

Five little kittens
Standing in a row,

They nod their heads
To the children, so.

They run to the left,
They run to the right,

They stand up and stretch
In the bright sunlight.

Along comes a dog,
Who's in for some fun.

Meow! See those
Five kittens run.

THE WHEELS ON THE BUS

The wheels on the bus
Go round and round,
Round and round,
Round and round.
The wheels on the bus
Go round and round
All over town!

Twirl
hands

The driver on the bus
Goes "Move to the rear!
Move to the rear!
Move to the rear!"
The driver on the bus
Goes "Move to the rear!"
All over town!

**The people on the bus
Go up and down,**
(and so on)

**The babies on the bus
Go "Wah! Wah! Wah!"**
(and so on)

**The mothers on the bus
Go "Shh, shh, shh,"**
(and so on)

(You can add other verses, too. Try "money goes
clink," "wipers go swish," and "children go yakkity-yak.")

WHERE IS THUMBKIN?

Where is Thumbkin?
Where is Thumbkin?

Here I am!

Here I am!

How are you today, sir?

Very well, I thank you.

Run away,

Run away.

(Repeat with all the fingers: Pointer, Tall Man,
Ring Man, and Pinkie.)

 # THE BEEHIVE

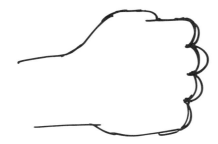

Here is the beehive.
Where are the bees?
Hidden away where nobody sees.
Watch as they come out of their hive—

| One, | Two, | Three, | Four, | Five! |

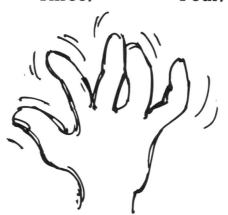

They're alive!
BZZZZ!

FIVE LITTLE MONKEYS

Five little monkeys
Jumping on the bed.

One fell off
And bumped his head.

Mama called the doctor,
And the doctor said,

shake finger

"That's what you get
For jumping on the bed!"

Four little monkeys . . .
(and so on)

Three little monkeys . . .
(and so on)

Two little monkeys . . .
(and so on)

One little monkey
Jumping on the bed.
He fell off
And bumped his head.
Mama called the doctor,
And the doctor said,
"No more monkeys
Jumping on the bed!"

TEN FAT PEAS

Ten fat peas in a peapod pressed.

One grew. . . . Two grew.   So did all the rest.

clap!

Until one day
The pod went POP!

They grew and grew   And did not stop

 # THE GRASSHOPPER

There was a little grasshopper

Who was always on the jump.

And because he never looked ahead,
He always got a bump.

IF YOU'RE HAPPY AND YOU KNOW IT

CLAP
TWICE
AFTER
SINGING
WORDS

CLAP
TWICE

If you're happy and you know it,
Clap your hands.

If you're happy and you know it,
Clap your hands.

CLAP
TWICE

If you're happy and you know it,
And you really want to show it,
If you're happy and you know it,
Clap your hands.

(Continue with other actions, such as stamp your
feet, touch your knees, nod your head, say
"Achoo!")

THE PEANUT SONG

Oh, a peanut sat
On a railroad track,

His heart was all a-flutter.

Along came the five-fifteen,

Uh-oh, peanut butter!

WHOOPS, JOHNNY!

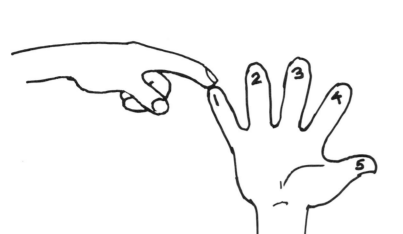

Johnny,

Johnny,

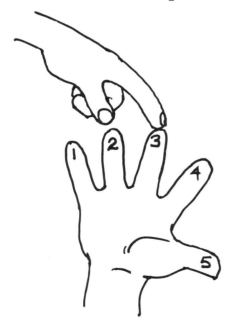

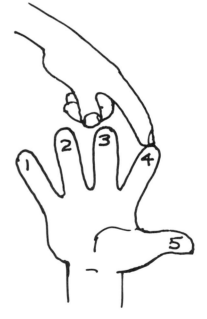

Johnny,

Johnny,

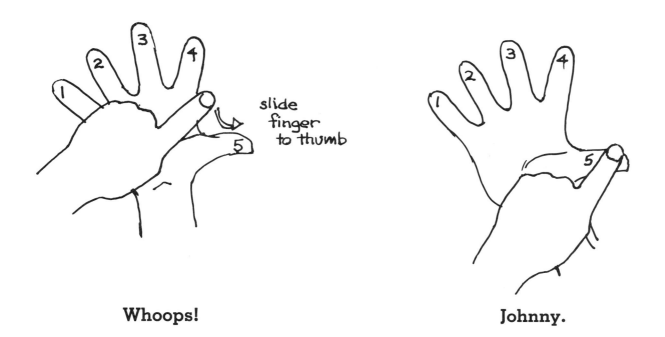

slide
finger
to thumb

Whoops!   Johnny.

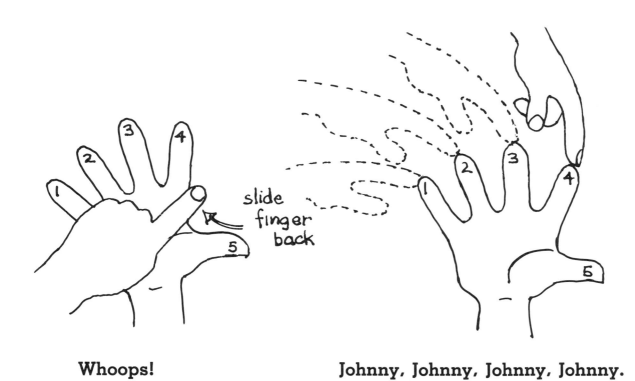

slide
finger
back

Whoops!   Johnny, Johnny, Johnny, Johnny.

THIS OLD MAN

Tap thumbs together

Tap Knees

This old man, he played one.

He played knick-knack
On his thumb.

With a knick-knack,

Clap! Clap!

"Throw" bone behind you

Twirl hands

This old man came
Rolling home.

Paddy-whack,

Give your dog a bone.

2nd Verse:

This old man, he played two.
He played knick-knack
On his shoe.
(and so on)

TOUCH SHOE

3rd Verse: "three" . . . "knee"

TOUCH KNEE

4th Verse: "four" . . . "door"

PRETEND TO KNOCK

5th Verse: "five" . . . "hive"

TAP FIST

6th Verse: "six" . . . "sticks"

TAP INDEX FINGERS TOGETHER

7th Verse: "seven" . . . "up to heaven"

POINT UP

8th Verse: "eight" . . . "gate"

TAP HAND

9th Verse: "nine" . . . "spine"

TAP SPINE

10th Verse: "ten" . . . "once again"

CLAP HANDS

TWO FAT GENTLEMEN

Two fat gentlemen
Met in a glen,

Bowed most politely,
Bowed once again.

Bend one

Bend the other

Bend both

How do you do? How do you do?
And how do you do again?

(Repeat with "two thin ladies" [index fingers]; "two
tall policemen" [middle fingers]; "two happy
schoolchildren" [ring fingers]; "two little babies"
[pinkies].)

CHOOK-CHOOK-CHOOK

Chook, chook, chook-chook-chook.
Good morning, Mrs. Hen.
How many children have you got?
Madam, I've got ten.

Four of them
Are yellow,

And four of them
Are brown,

And two of them
Are speckled red—
The nicest in the town!

THE ELEPHANT

The elephant goes like this and that.

He's oh, so big,
And he's oh, so fat.

He has no fingers,
And he has no toes,

But goodness gracious,
What a nose!

BIRTHDAY CAKE

Ten candles on a birthday cake,

All lit up for me.

I'll make a wish and blow them out.

Blow and bend fingers down

Watch and you will see.
Whhh!

ON MY HEAD

On my head my hands I place.   On my shoulders,   On my face,

On my hips,   And at my side,

Then behind me they will hide.

I will hold them up so high,
Quickly make my fingers fly,

Hold them out in front of me,

Swiftly clap them—
One, two, three.

TEN IN THE BED

There were ten in the bed,

And the little one said,
"Roll over! Roll over!"

So they all rolled over,
And one fell out.

There were nine in the bed,
(and so on)

There were eight in the bed. . . .

There were seven in the bed. . . .

There were six in the bed. . . .

There were five in the bed. . . .

There were four in the bed. . . .

There were three in the bed. . . .

There were two in the bed. . . .

There was one in the bed,
And the little one said,
"Good night!"

MUSICAL ARRANGEMENTS

SIX LITTLE DUCKS
(see pages 10-11)

OPEN, SHUT THEM

(see pages 12-13)

O - pen, Shut them. O - pen, Shut them. Give a lit - tle clap.

O - pen, Shut them. O - pen, Shut them. Place them in your lap.

Creep them, creep them. Creep them, creep them Right up to your chin.

O - pen wide your lit - tle mouth, But do not let them in.

I'M A LITTLE TEAPOT

(see page 20)

I'm a lit - tle tea - pot, Short and stout.

Here is my han - dle, Here is my spout. When I get all steamed up,

Hear me shout, "Tip me o - ver and pour me out!"

BLUEBIRDS
(see page 22)

Two lit - tle blue - birds Sit - ting on a hill,

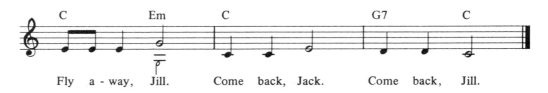

One named Jack, The oth - er named Jill. Fly a - way, Jack.

Fly a - way, Jill. Come back, Jack. Come back, Jill.

THE EENTSY, WEENTSY SPIDER
(see page 25)

The een - tsy, ween - tsy spi - der Climbed up the wa - ter - spout.

Down came the rain And washed the spi - der out.

Out came the sun And dried up all the rain. And the

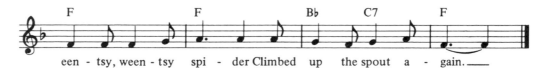

een - tsy, ween - tsy spi - der Climbed up the spout a - gain.

THE HAMMER SONG

(see pages 30-31)

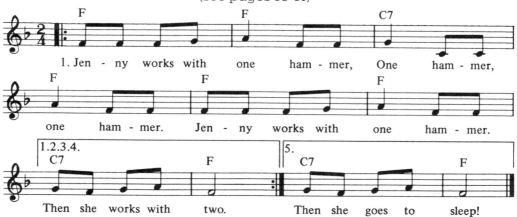

1. Jen - ny works with one ham - mer, One ham - mer,
one ham - mer. Jen - ny works with one ham - mer.

1.2.3.4. Then she works with two.

5. Then she goes to sleep!

2. Jenny works with two hammers, Two hammers, two hammers. Jenny works with two hammers. Then she works with three.

3. Jenny works with three hammers, Three hammers, three hammers. Jenny works with three hammers. Then she works with four.

4. Jenny works with four hammers, Four hammers, four hammers. Jenny works with four hammers. Then she works with five.

5. Jenny works with five hammers, Five hammers, five hammers. Jenny works with five hammers. Then she goes to sleep!

THE WHEELS ON THE BUS

(see pages 34-35)

1. The wheels on the bus Go round and round,
2. (The) driv - er on the bus Goes "Move to the rear!

Round and round, Round and round. The
Move to the rear! Move to the rear!" The

wheels on the bus Go round and round
driv - er on the bus Goes "Move to the rear!"

1.2. etc. All o - ver town!_____ 2. The _____
All o - ver town!_____ 3. The _____

Last time

3. The people on the bus Go up and down, (etc.)
4. The babies on the bus Go "Wah! Wah! Wah!" (etc.)
5. The mothers on the bus Go "Shh, shh, shh," (etc.)

Note: You can add other verses, too. Try, "money goes clink," "wipers go swish," and "children go yakkity-yak."

— **59** —

WHERE IS THUMBKIN?

(see page 36)

Where is Thumb - kin? Where is Thumb - kin?

Here I am! Here I am! How are you to - day, sir?

Ver - y well, I thank you. Run a - way, Run a - way.

(Repeat with all the fingers: Pointer, Tall Man, Ring Man, and Pinkie.)

IF YOU'RE HAPPY AND YOU KNOW IT

(see page 42)

If you're hap - py and you know it, Clap your hands. If you're

hap - py and you know it, Clap your hands. If you're

hap - py and you know it, And you real - ly want to show it, If you're

hap - py and you know it, Clap your hands.

(Continue with other actions, such as stamp your feet, nod your head, say "Achoo!")

THE PEANUT SONG

(see page 43)

Oh, a pea - nut sat On a rail - road track, His

heart was all a - flut - ter. A - long came the

five - fif - teen, Uh - oh, pea - nut but - ter!

THIS OLD MAN

(see pages 46-47)

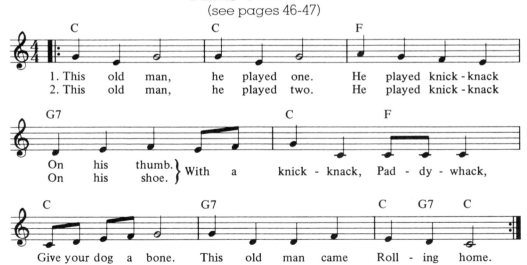

1. This old man, he played one. He played knick - knack
2. This old man, he played two. He played knick - knack

On his thumb. } With a knick - knack, Pad - dy - whack,
On his shoe.

Give your dog a bone. This old man came Roll - ing home.

ADDITIONAL VERSES:

3rd verse: "three" . . . "knee"	7th verse: "seven" . . . "up to heaven"
4th verse: "four" . . . "door"	8th verse: "eight" . . . "gate"
5th verse: "five" . . . "hive"	9th verse: "nine" . . . "spine"
6th verse: "six" . . . "sticks"	10th verse: "ten" . . . "once again"

TEN IN THE BED

(see pages 54-55)

There were ten in the bed, And the lit - tle one said, "Roll

(Repeat through "two in the bed,")

o - ver! Roll o - ver!" So they all rolled o - ver, And

one fell out. There were nine* in the bed, And the

(Repeat 7 times)

lit - tle one said, "Roll o - ver! Roll o - ver!" So they

(Last time only)

all rolled o - ver, And one fell out. There was

one in the bed, And the lit - tle one said, *(spoken)* "Good night!"

*Eight in the bed, etc.
Continue until "two in the bed,"
then end with "Last time only" section.

WHERE TO FIND MORE

SOME SOURCES FOR FINGERPLAYS AND ACTION RHYMES

Brown, Marc. *Finger Rhymes*. New York: E. P. Dutton, 1980.

———. *Hand Rhymes*. New York: E. P. Dutton, 1985.

———. *Play Rhymes*. New York: E. P. Dutton, 1987.

Delamar, Gloria T. *Children's Counting-Out Rhymes, Fingerplays, Jump-Rope and Ball-Bounce Chants, and Other Rhythms*. Jefferson, N.C.: McFarland, 1983.

Emerson, Sally. *The Nursery Treasury*. New York: Doubleday, 1988.

Glazer, Tom. *Music for Ones and Twos*. Garden City, N.Y.: Doubleday, 1983.

———. *Eye Winker, Tom Tinker, Chin Chopper*. Garden City, N.Y.: Doubleday, 1973.

Grayson, Marion. *Let's Do Fingerplays*. Washington, D.C.: Robert B. Luce, 1962.

Hayes, Sarah. *Clap Your Hands*. New York: Lothrop, Lee & Shepard, 1988.

Jacobs, E. Frances. *Finger Plays and Action Rhymes*. New York: Lothrop, Lee and Shepard, 1941.

Matterson, Elizabeth. *Games for the Very Young*. New York: American Heritage Press, 1969.

Pooley, Sarah. *A Day of Rhymes*. New York: Alfred A. Knopf, 1987.

Poulsson, Emilie. *Finger Plays for Nursery and Kindergarten*. Boston: Lothrop, Lee and Shepard, 1893.

INDEX OF FIRST LINES

ORIGO
STEPPING STONES
CORE MATHEMATICS

SENIOR AUTHORS

Rosemary Irons

James Burnett

CONTRIBUTING AUTHORS

Peter Stowasser

Allan Turton

PROGRAM CONSULTANTS

Diana Lambdin

Frank Lester, Jr.

Kit Norris

PROGRAM EDITORS

James Burnett

Beth Lewis

Donna Richards

Kevin Young

ORIGO
EDUCATION

PRACTICE BOOK

ORIGO STEPPING STONES

The *ORIGO Stepping Stones* program has been created to provide a smarter way to teach and learn mathematics. It has been developed by a team of experts to provide a world-class math program.

PRACTICE BOOK

Regular and meaningful practice is a hallmark of *ORIGO Stepping Stones*. Each module in this practice book has pages that revisit content from an earlier module to maintain concepts and skills, and pages that practice numeral writing or computation to promote fluency.

PERFORATED PAGES

Young students need many hands-on experiences to sort, match, compare, and order quantities, pictures, words, and numerals long before they can write. The perforation in this book allows students to remove and cut out images for use in activities such as these.

Space for the student's name when a page is removed.

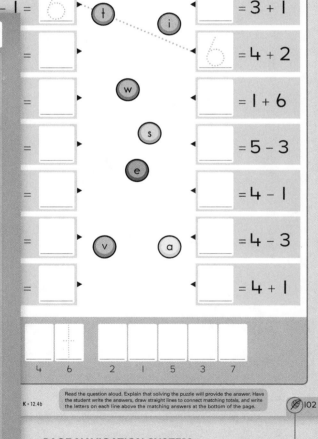

ants

more ant

ants in total

ladybugs

more ladybugs

ladybugs in total

bees

more bees

bees in total

butterflies

more butterflies

butterflies in total

For each picture, have the student write the number in each group, then write the total.

ORIGO Stepping Stones **K** • 7.1   52

How does the sea say hello?

$7 - 1 = 6$

$= 3 + 1$

$= 4 + 2$

$= 1 + 6$

$= 5 - 3$

$= 4 - 1$

$= 4 - 3$

$= 4 + 1$

4   6   2   1   5   3   7

K • 12.4b   Read the question aloud. Explain that solving the puzzle will provide the answer. Have the student write the answers, draw straight lines to connect matching totals, and write the letters on each line above the matching answers at the bottom of the page.   102

ORIGO Stepping Stones **K** • 7.1

Grade   Module   Lesson

PAGE NAVIGATION SYSTEM

Most users of this book have not yet learned to read two-digit numbers. This book provides a special navigation symbol at the bottom of each page. There is one unique symbol for each module. The color of the symbol indicates the position of the lesson in the module. Rather than asking students to turn to a page number, the teacher can say, "Turn to the pink apple."

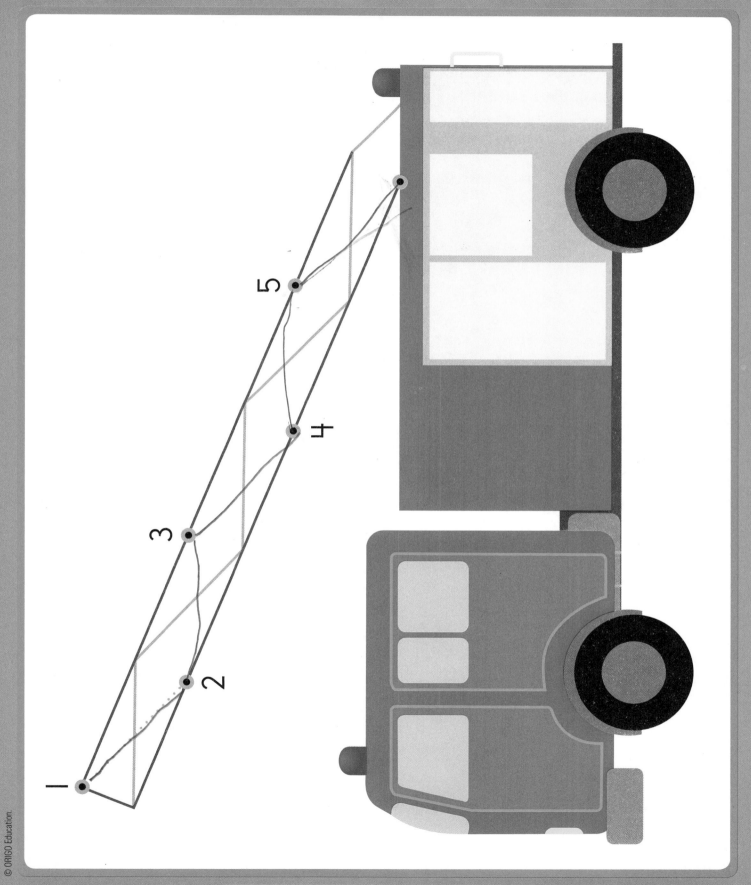

Have the student draw lines from 1 to 5 while saying the numbers aloud.

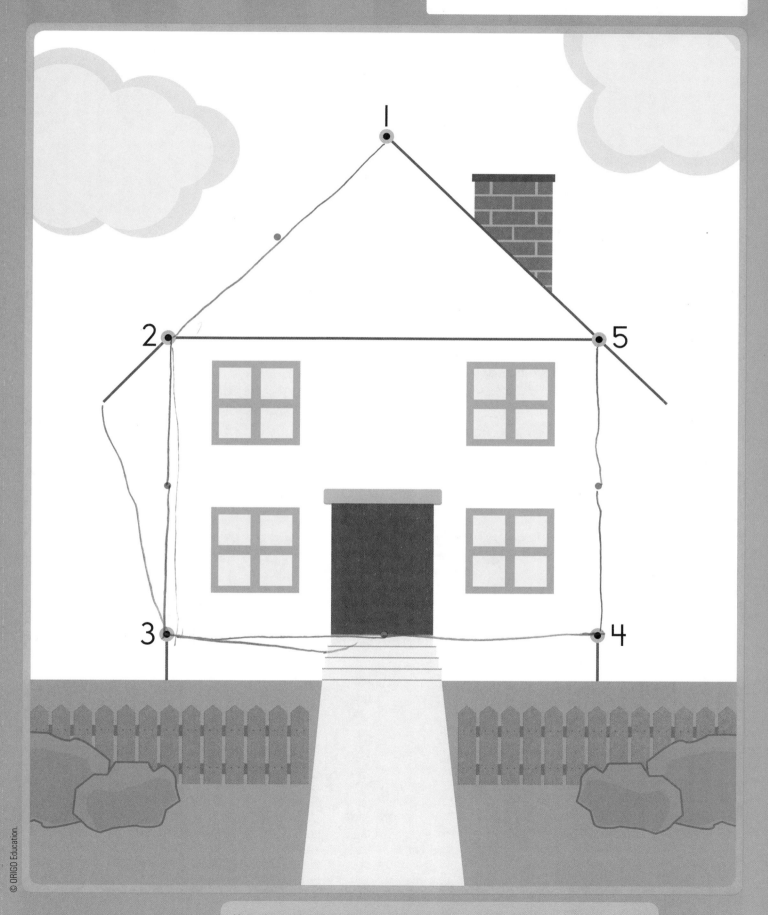

Have the student draw lines from 1 to 5 while saying the numbers aloud.
They can pause on the red halfway points if necessary.

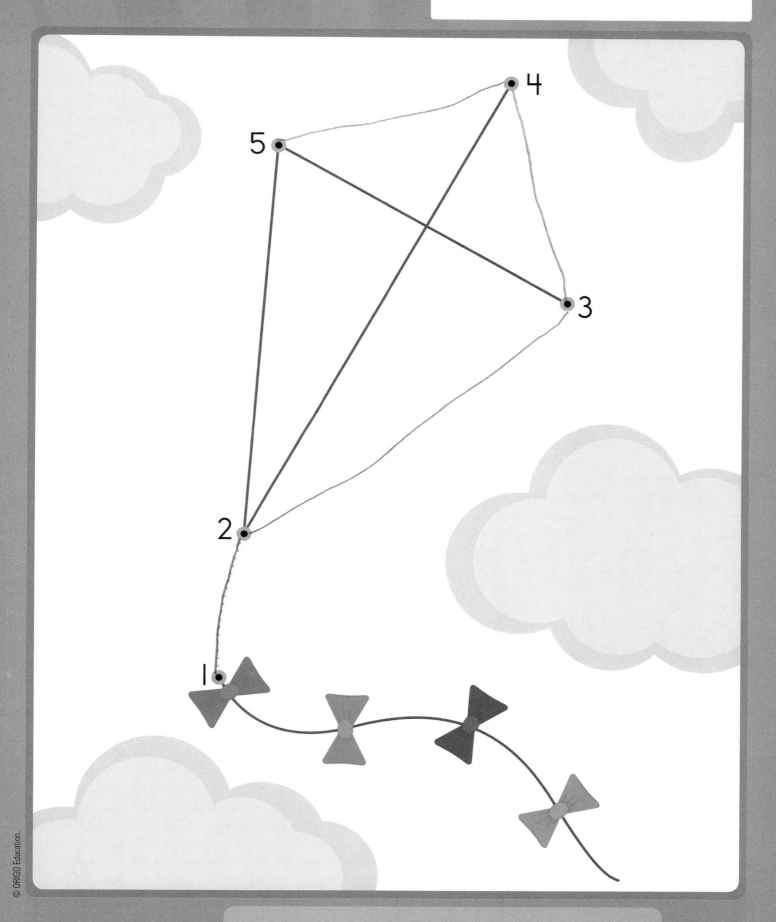

Have the student draw lines from 1 to 5 while saying the numbers aloud.

3

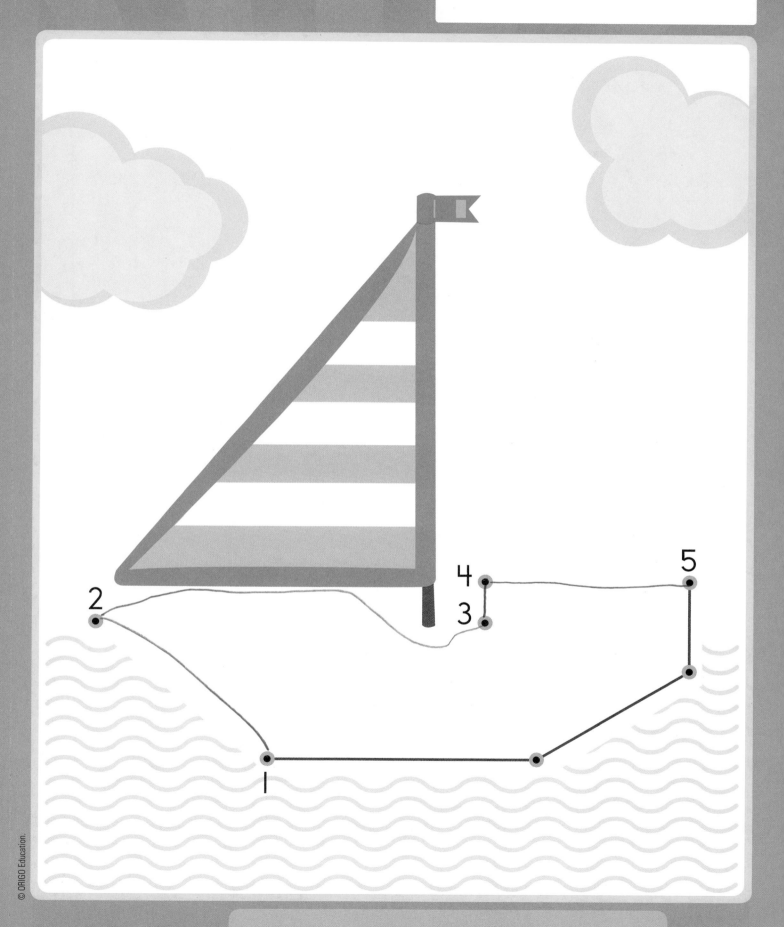

Have the student draw lines from 1 to 5 while saying the numbers aloud.

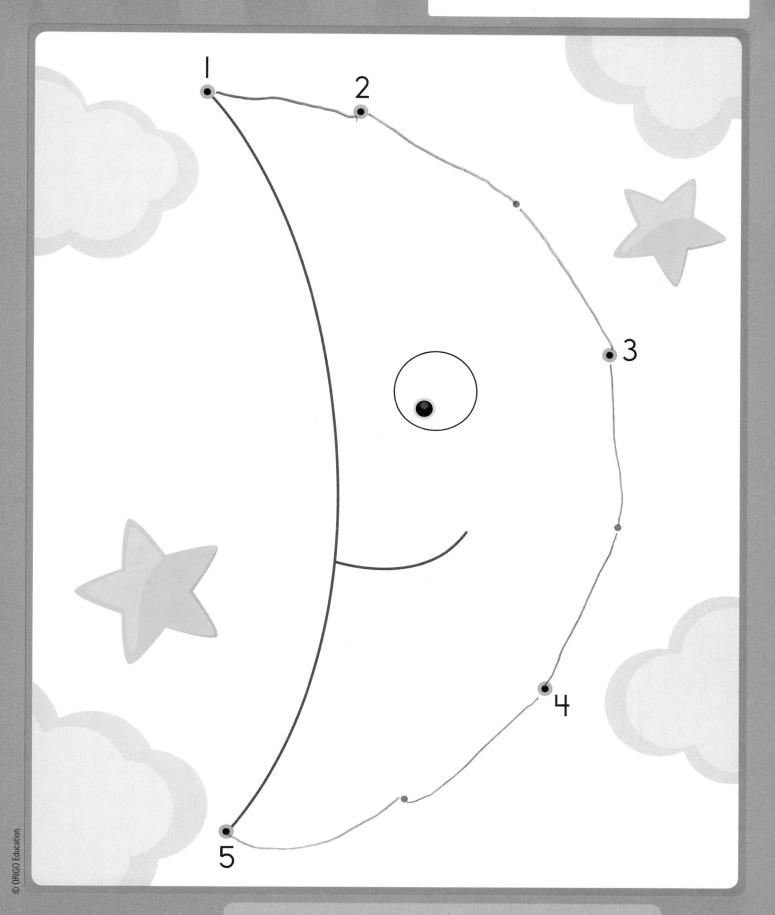

Have the student draw lines from 1 to 5 while saying the numbers aloud.
They can pause at the red halfway points if necessary.

5

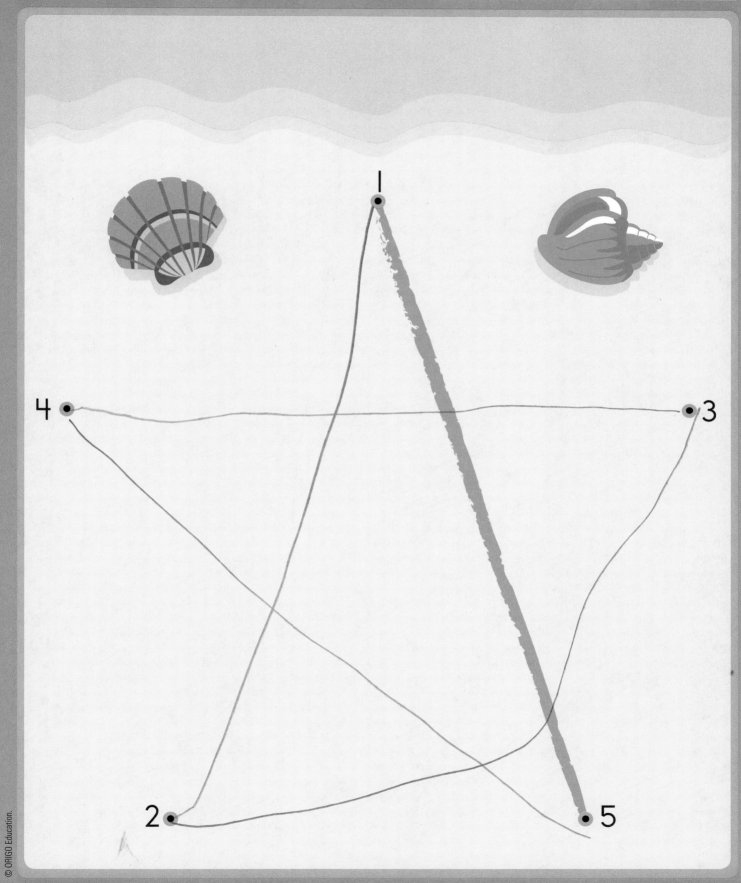

Have the student draw a line in the sand from 1 to 5 while saying the numbers aloud.

how many bay

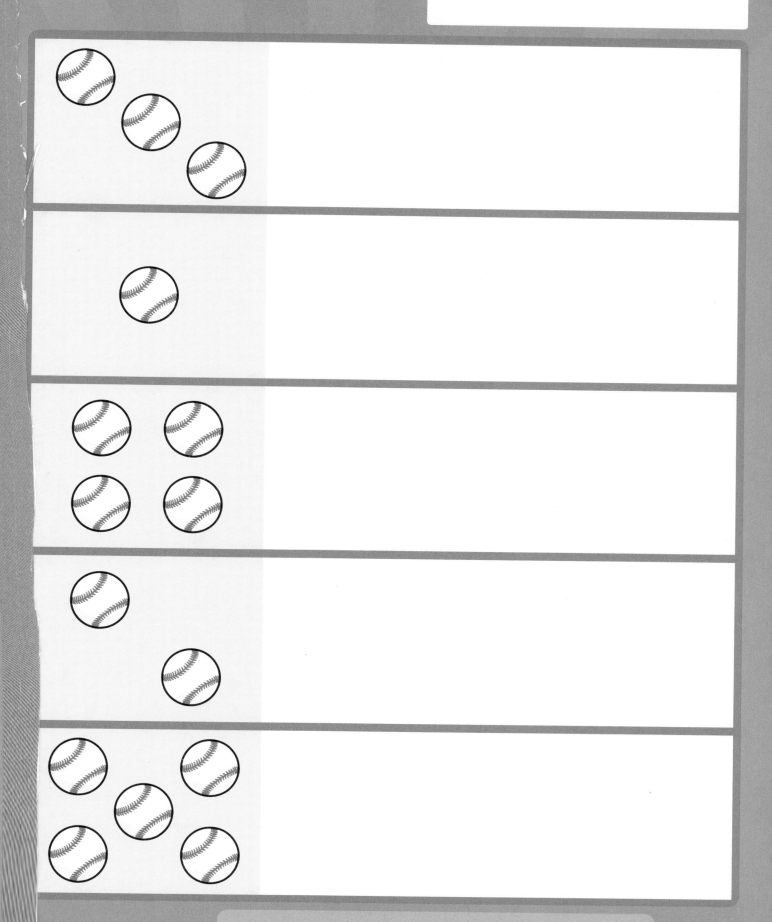

Have the student place and trace around counters to match the quantity of baseballs as shown. Ask the student to count each group aloud.

ORIGO Stepping Stones K • 2.2b

Have the student draw lines from 1 to 10 while saying the numbers aloud.

9

2

5

1

4

3

Have the student place and trace around counters to match the numeral. Ask the student to draw a face (☺) on each and count aloud the number in each group.

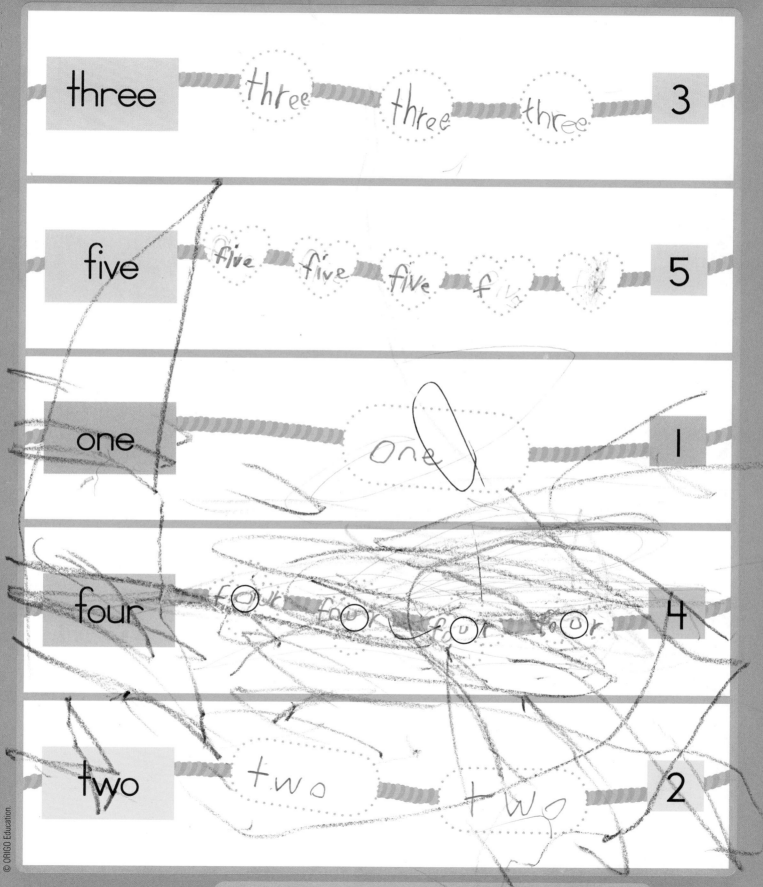

three   three   three   three   **3**

five   five   five   five   **5**

one   one   **1**

four   four   four   four   four   **4**

two   two   two   **2**

Have the student draw and color beads to match the number name and numeral.
Ask the student to read, count, and say the number of beads on each thread.

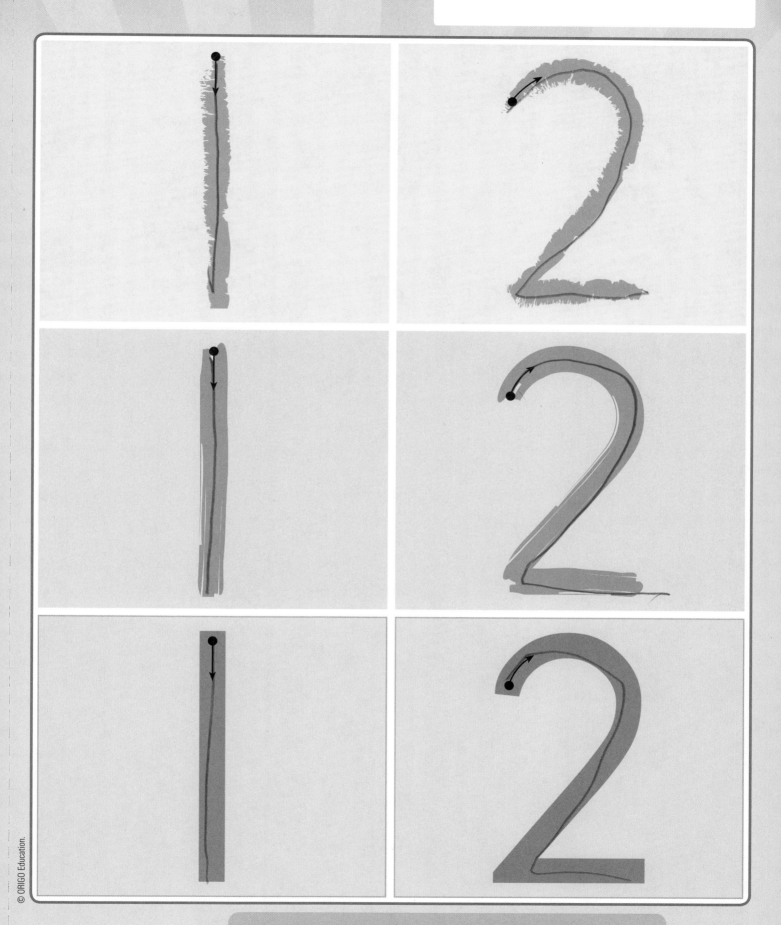

Have the student read each number aloud, trace over it with their finger, then write each numeral three times.

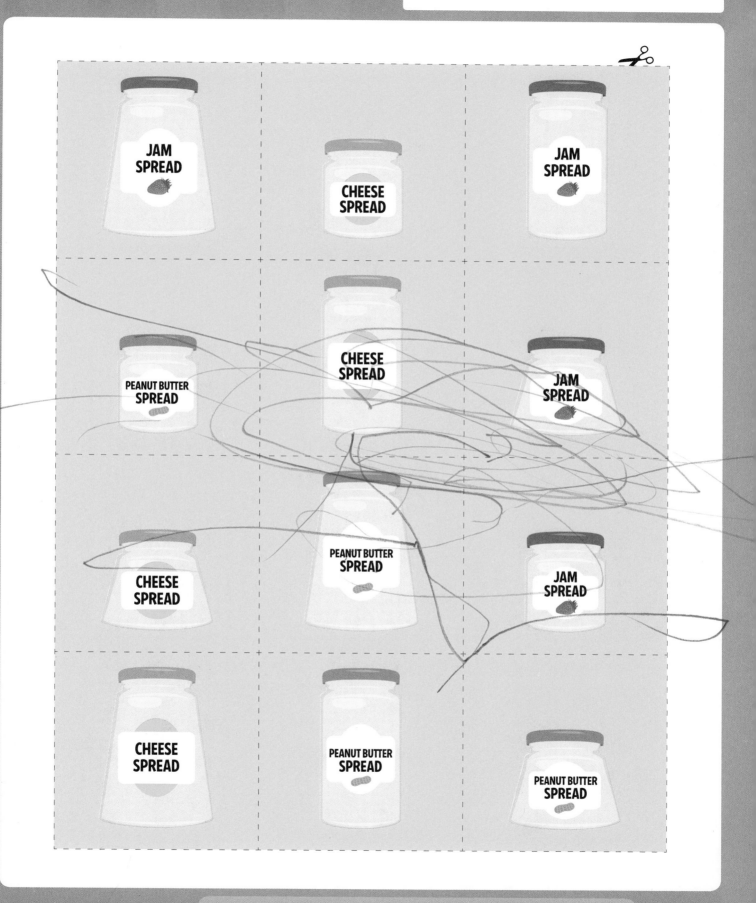

Read the labels aloud. Have the student cut out and sort the pictures into **two** groups, then describe their sort. Ask the student to sort in another way. Have the student paste one of their sorts onto a sheet of paper.

Have the student cut out and sort the pictures into groups, describe their sort, then sort in another way. Have the student paste one of their sorts onto a sheet of paper.

Have the student read each number aloud, trace over it with their finger,
then write each numeral three times.

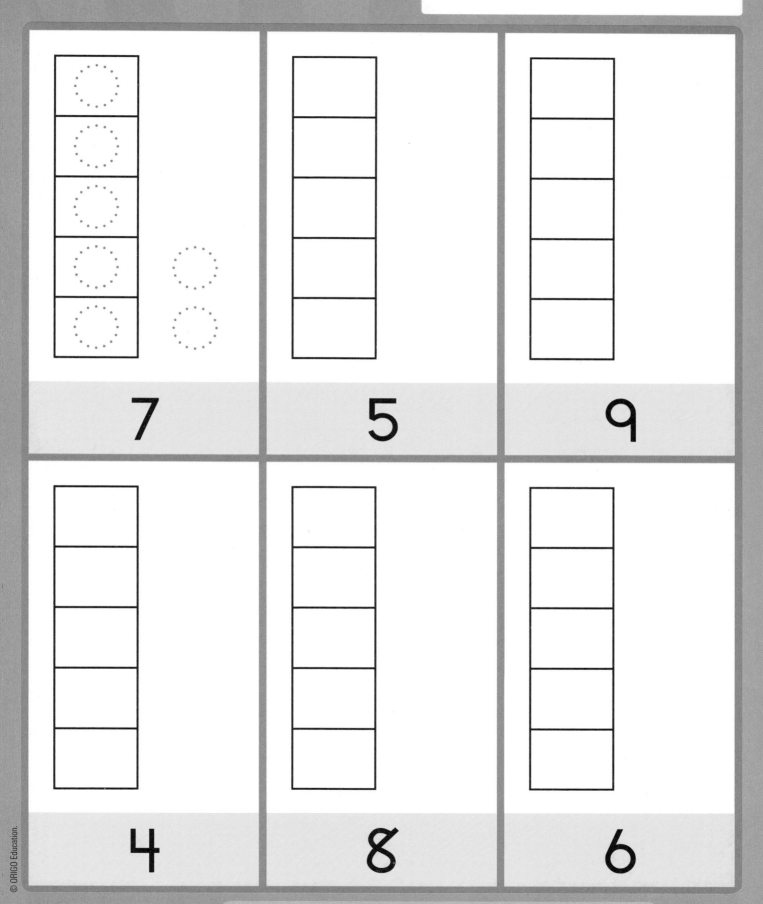

7

5

9

4

8

6

Have the student draw counters (○) to match the numeral, filling in the five-frame first. Ask the student to describe each one as "Seven is five and two more" and so on.

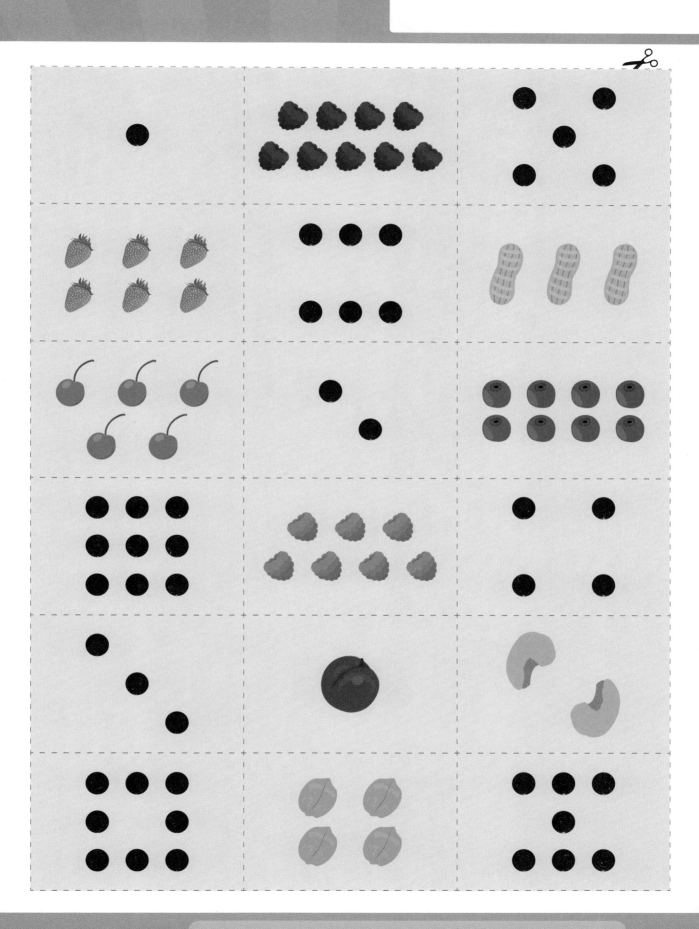

Have the student cut out the pictures and paste matching quantities back-to-back.

Have the student read each number aloud, trace over it with their finger,
then write each numeral three times.

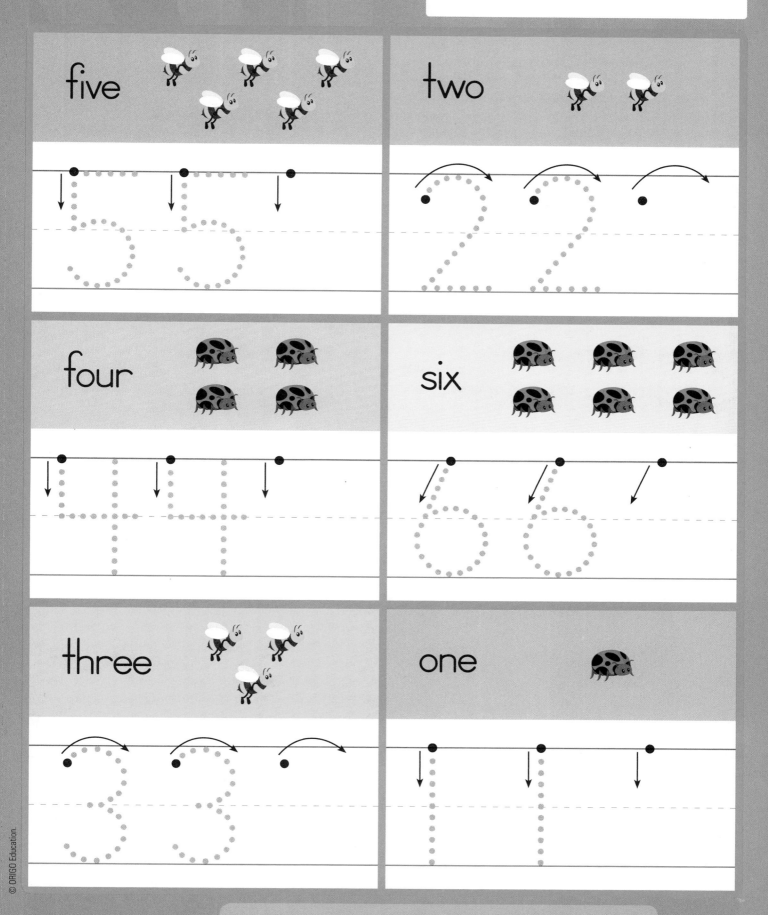

five

two

four

six

three

one

Have the student read the word and count the bugs, then follow the arrows
to write the matching numerals.

19

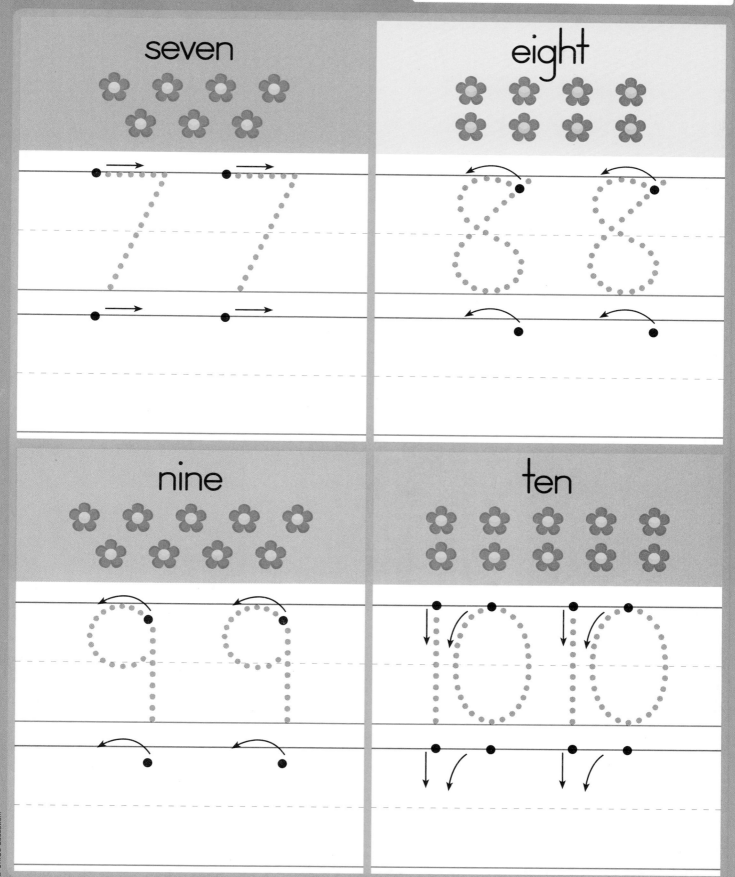

seven

eight

nine

ten

Have the student read the word and count the flowers, then follow the arrow to write the matching numerals.

Have the student read each number aloud, trace over it with their finger, then write each numeral three times.

Have the student complete the missing pieces of the puzzles.

yes	no

Have the student cut out the face pictures, ask seven people the question
"Are dogs your favorite pet?" then paste the faces in the appropriate columns.

23

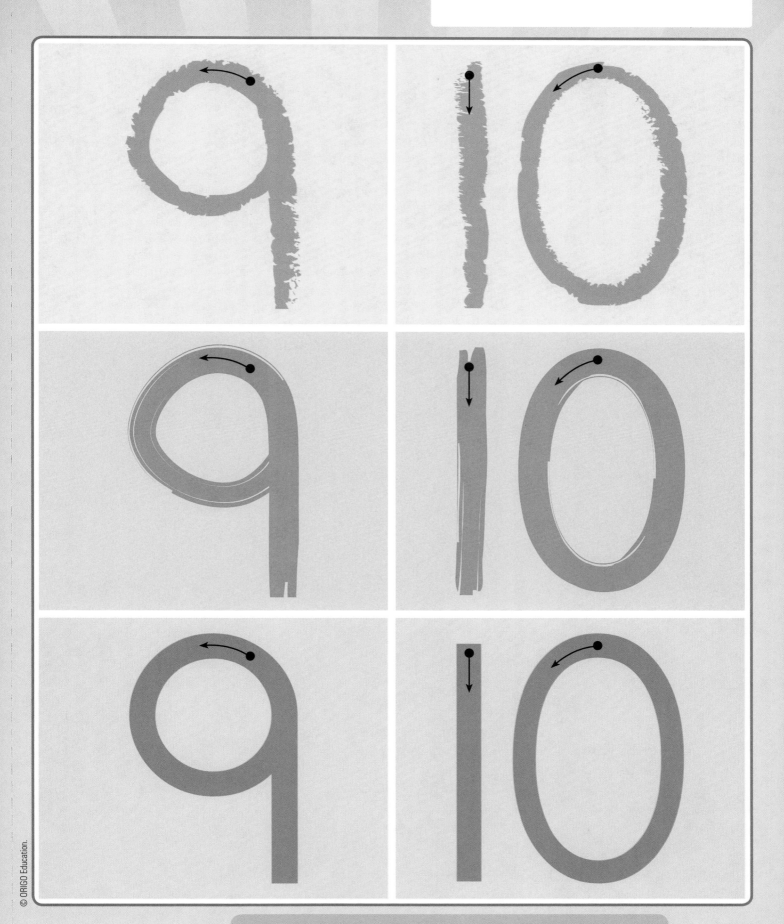

Have the student read each number aloud, trace over it with their finger, then write each numeral three times.

Have the student say the number of dots in each group then write the numeral.

1 2 ___ ___ ___ 6 7 8 9 10

1 2 3 4 ___ ___ ___ 8 9 10

___ ___ ___ 4 5 6 7 8 9 10

1 2 3 4 5 6 ___ ___ ___ 10

Have the student work left to right to trace over the gray numerals
and write the missing numerals on each number track.

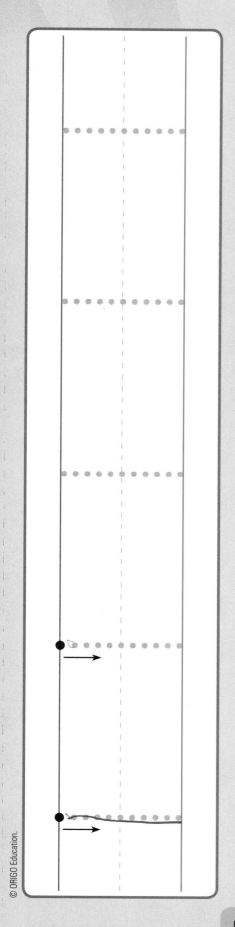

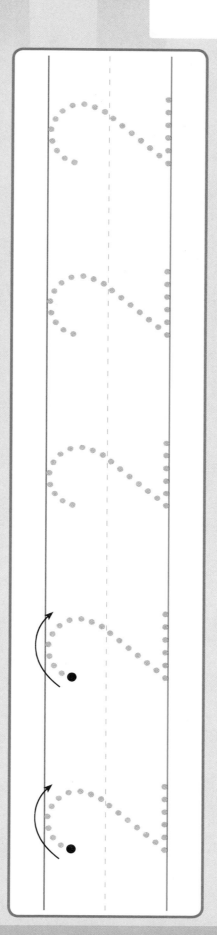

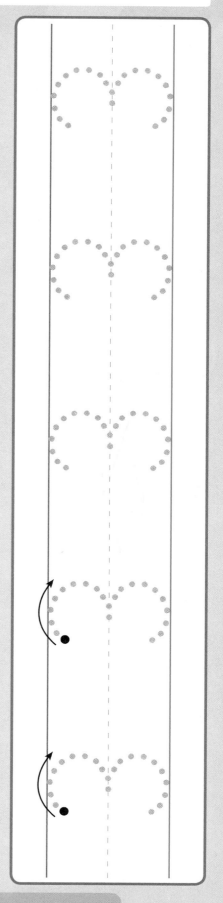

Have the student read the first numeral then trace it five times.
Repeat for the other numerals.

27

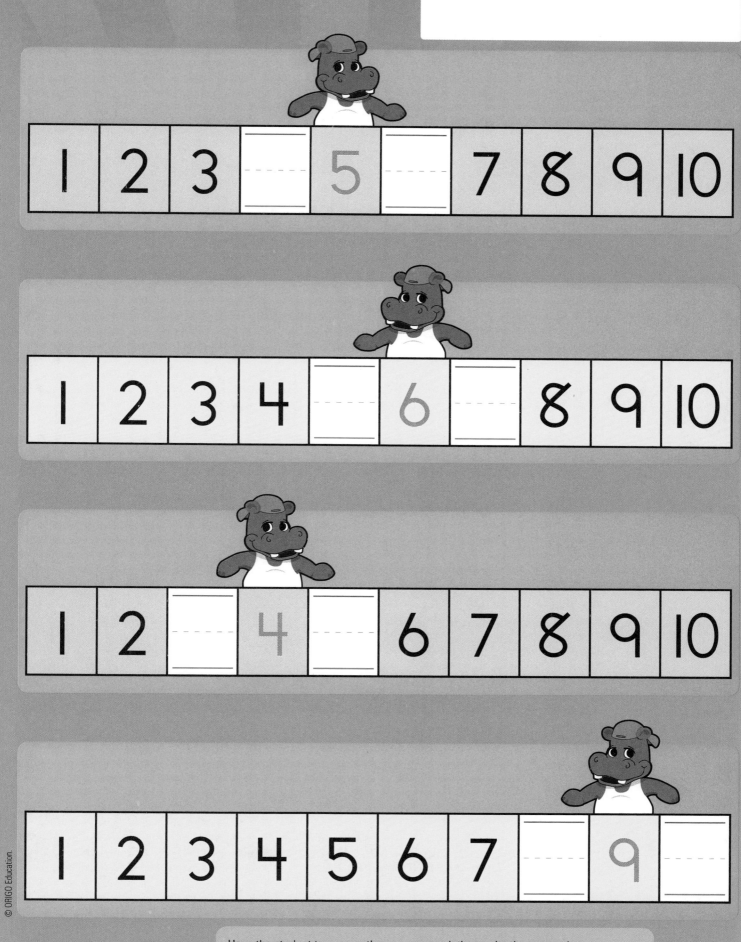

Have the student trace over the gray numeral, then write the numerals that are just before and just after.

just before

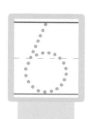

just after

Have the student trace over the words then write the appropriate numerals.
They can use the number track to help.

29

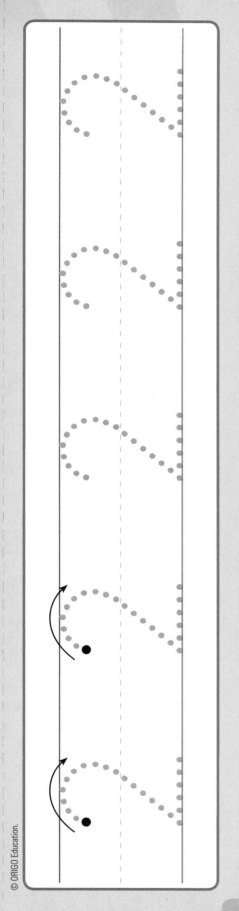
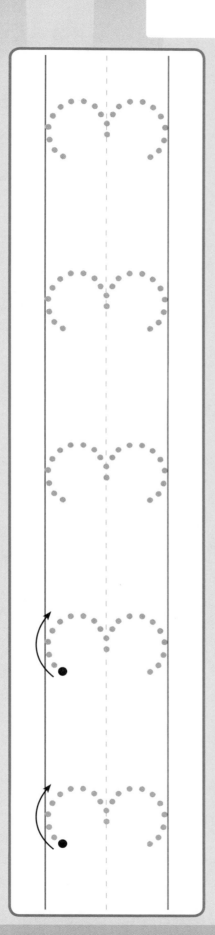
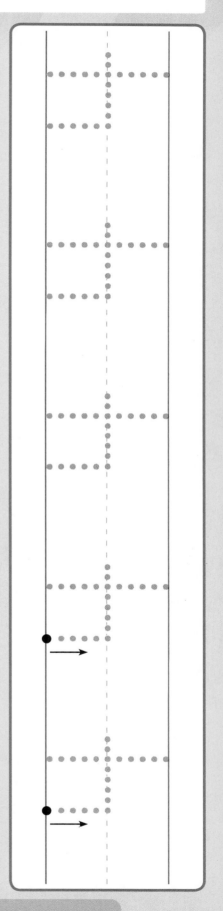

Have the student read the first numeral then trace it five times.
Repeat for the other numerals.

ORIGO Stepping Stones **K** • 4.4b

30

Draw a 🌸 **beside** the tree.

Draw a 🐦 **on top of** the swing.

Draw a ◯ **next to** the dog.

Draw a ☼ **above** the clouds.

Draw a ⛑ **below** the swing.

ORIGO Stepping Stones **K** • 4.5

Read each instruction aloud. Have the student draw each picture in the correct position.

31

Have the student color each astronaut's left hand and left foot.

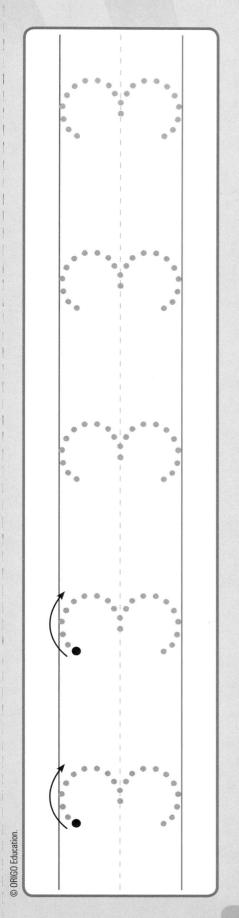

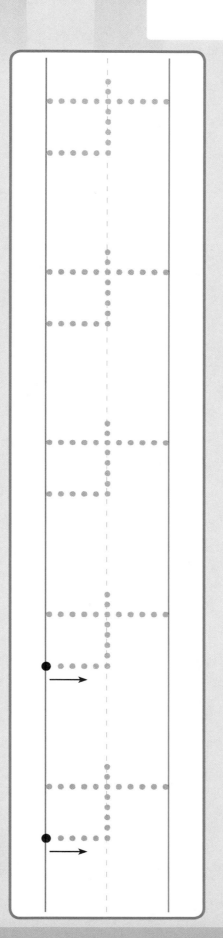

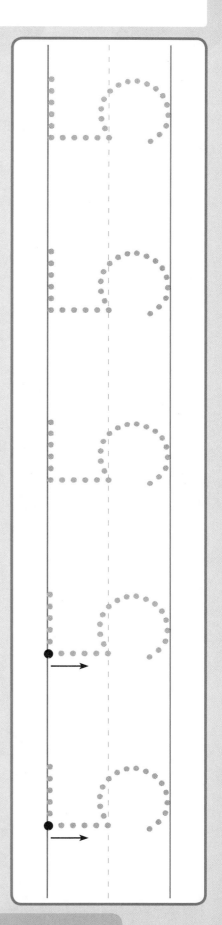

Have the student read the first numeral then trace it five times.
Repeat for the other numerals.

less than		greater than

Have the student say the number in each group, then draw pictures that show quantities less than and greater than each group.

a.

b.

c.

d.

For each puzzle, have the student write the numbers of fingers raised, then draw a line around the greater numeral.

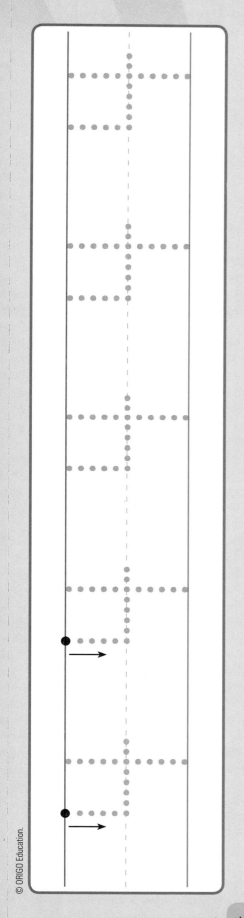
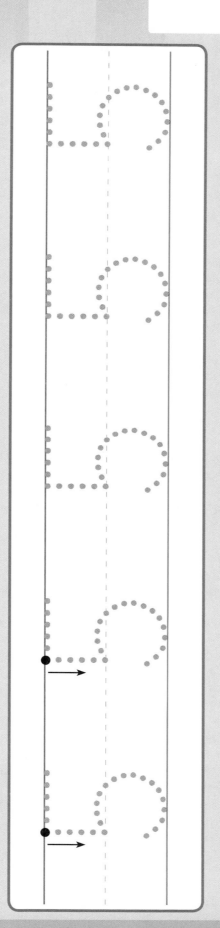
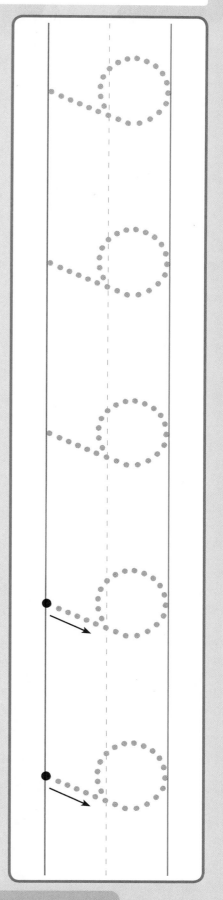

ORIGO Stepping Stones **K** • 5.2b

Have the student read the first numeral then trace it five times.
Repeat for the other numerals.

© ORIGO Education.

b.

c.

d.

e.

f.

For each of these, have the student write the numbers of dots, then draw a line around the group of dots that is less.

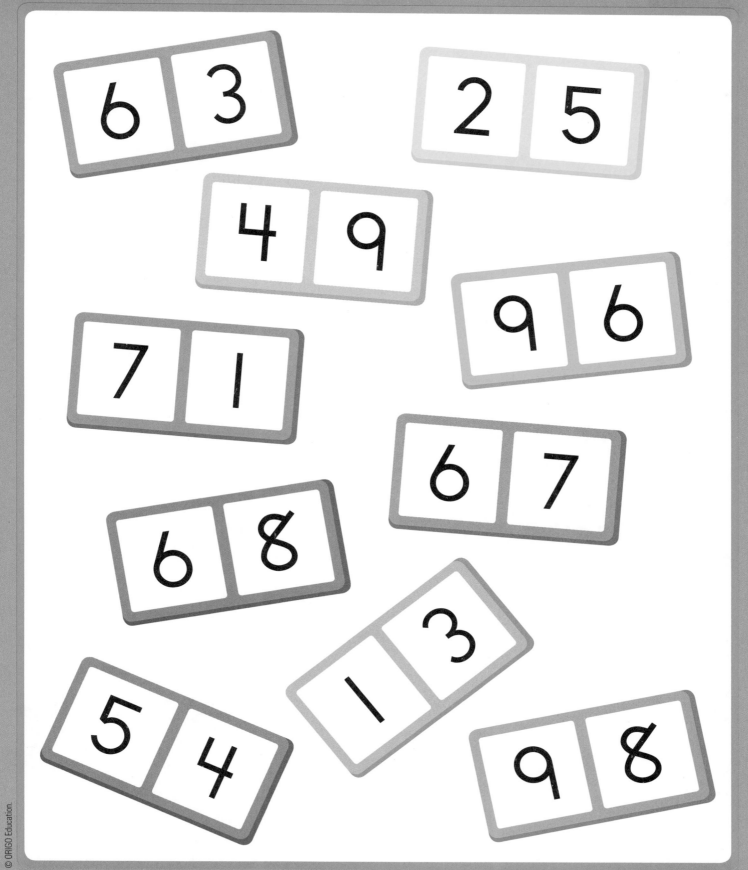

Have the student read aloud the two numerals on a card then color the greater numeral. Repeat for all.

38

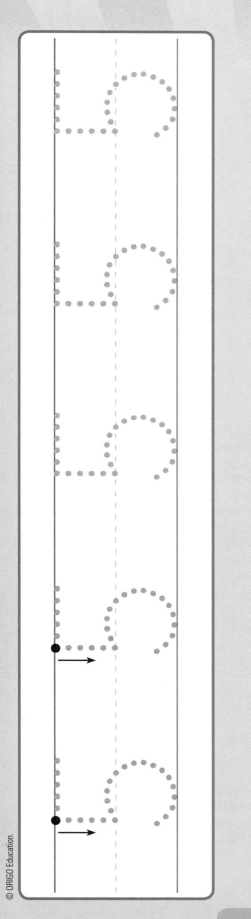
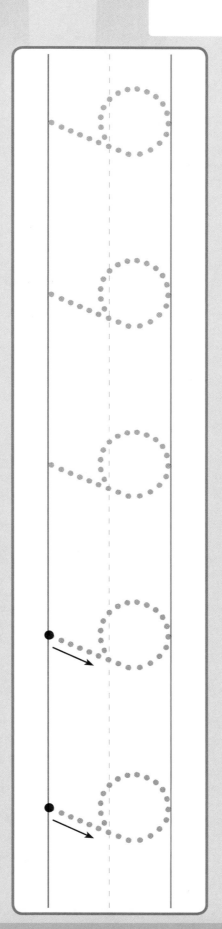
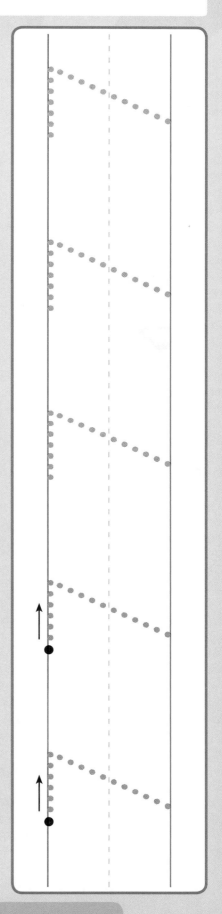

ORIGO Stepping Stones K • 5.4b

Have the student read the first numeral then trace it five times.
Repeat for the other numerals.

39

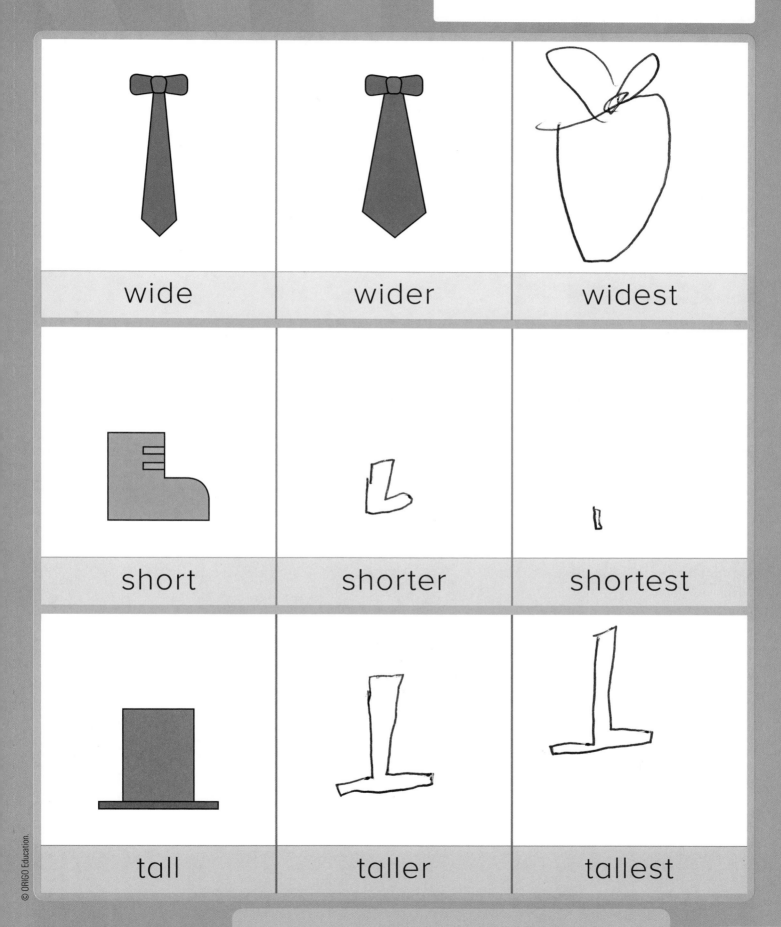

wide	wider	widest
short	shorter	shortest
tall	taller	tallest

Have the student draw a tie, boots, and hats to match the labels.

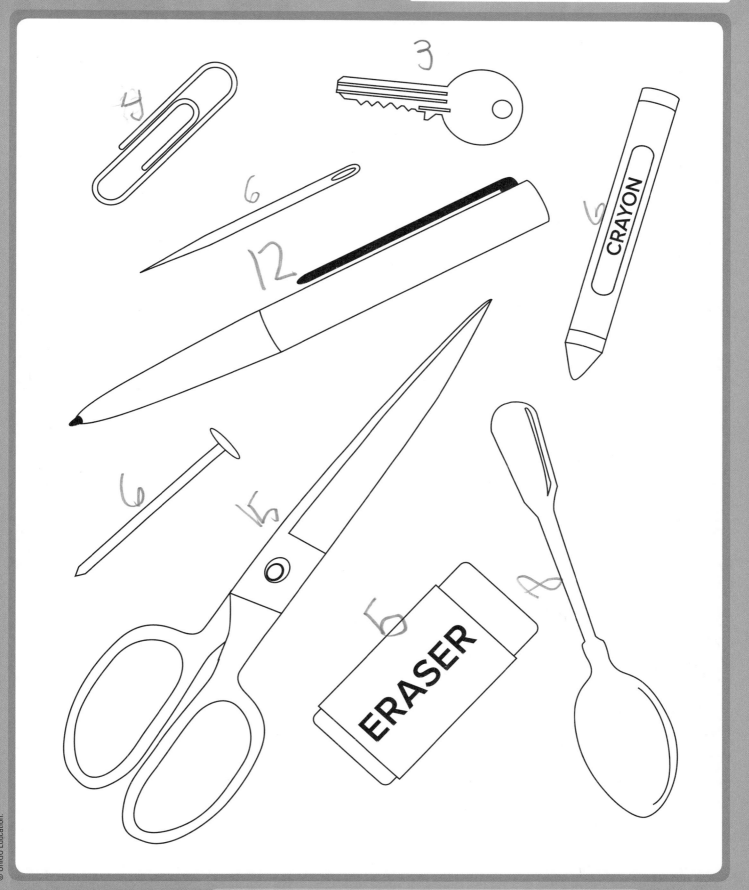

Cut a piece of string 4 inches long. Have the student compare the string to each picture, then color blue the pictures that are shorter and color red the pictures that are longer.

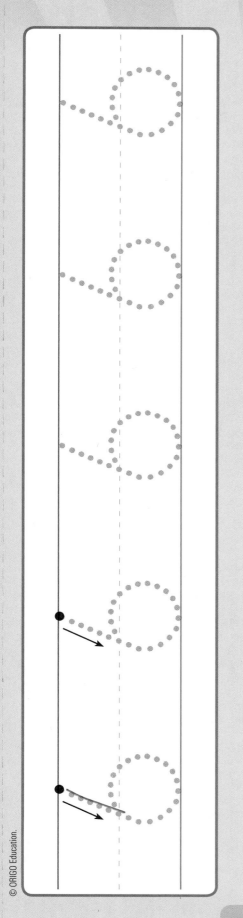
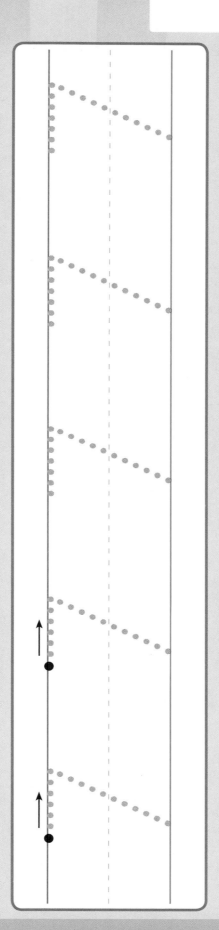
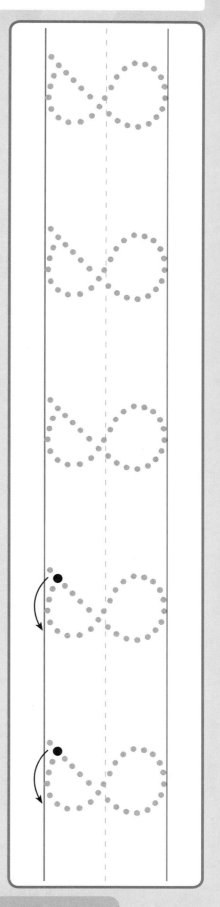

ORIGO Stepping Stones K • 5.6b

Have the student read the first numeral then trace it five times.
Repeat for the other numerals.

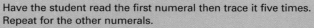 42

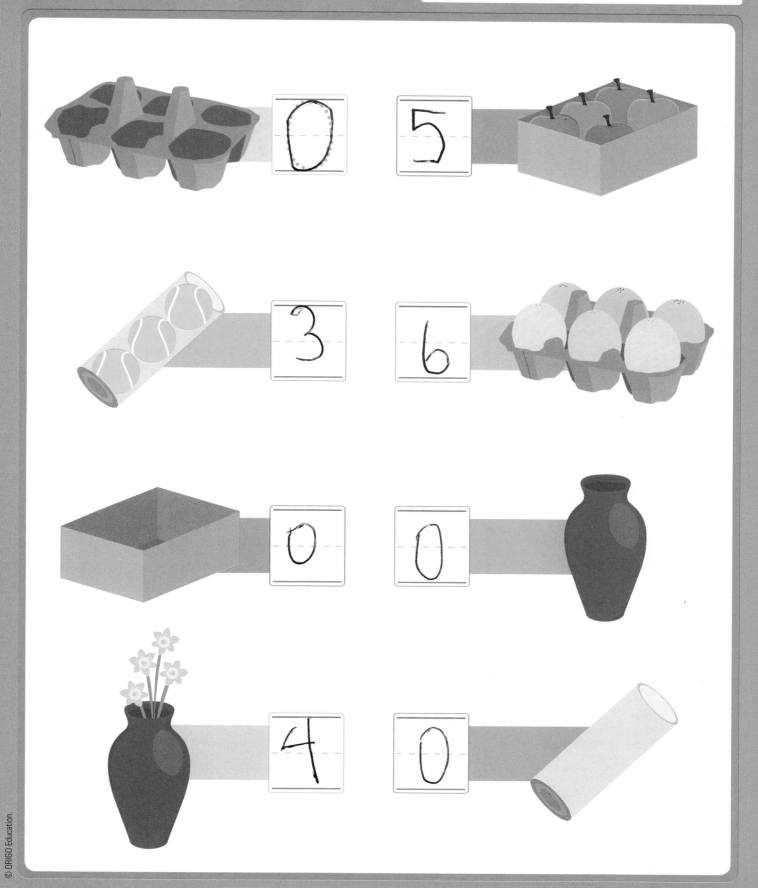

Have the student write the numeral to match the number they see in each.

four	seven	ten
one	zero	three
six	five	eight
nine	two	

Have the student cut out the pictures, paste matching pairs together on a sheet of paper, and write the matching numeral for each pair.

44

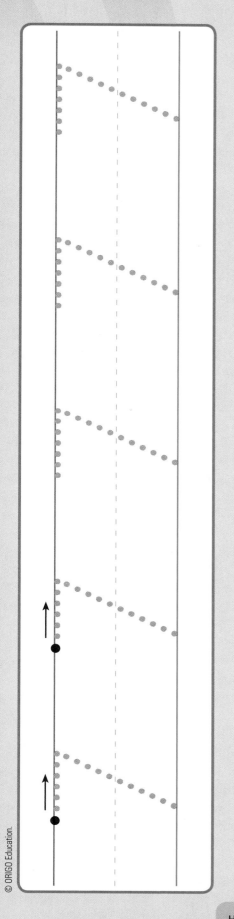
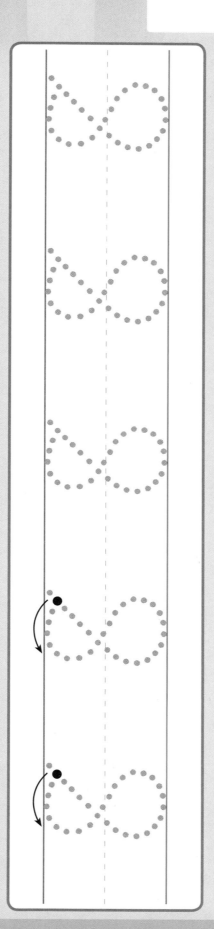
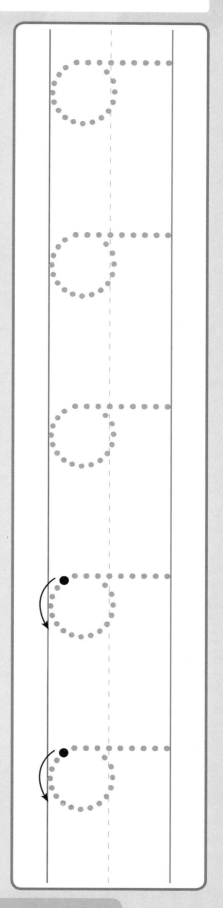

Have the student read the first numeral then trace it five times.
Repeat for the other numerals.

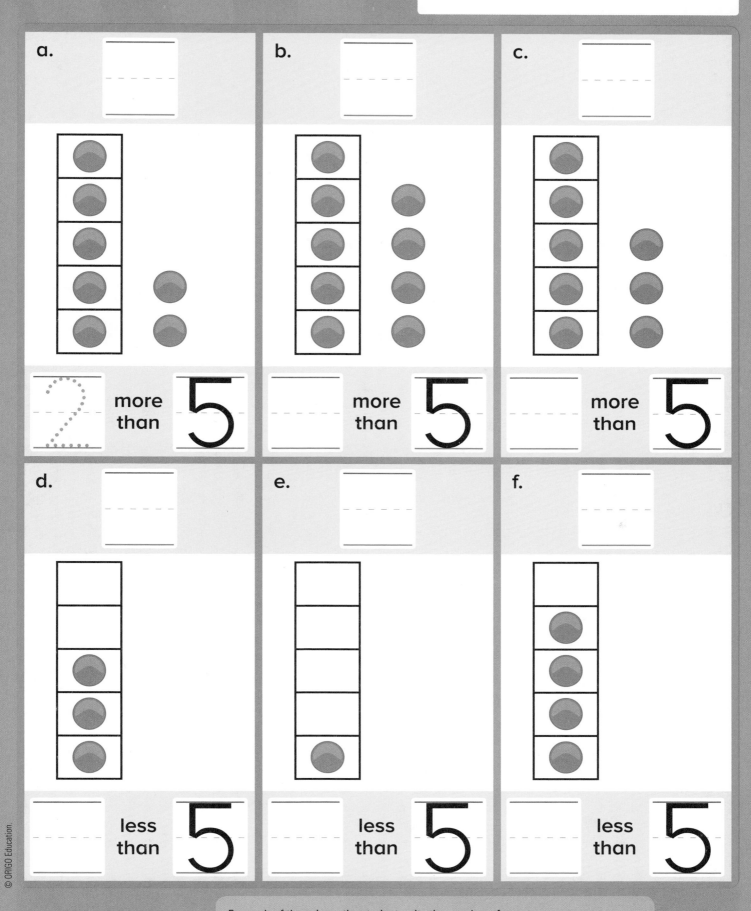

a.

more than **5**

b.

more than **5**

c.

more than **5**

d.

less than **5**

e.

less than **5**

f.

less than **5**

For each of these have the student write the number of counters then complete the comparison.

Have the student draw counters (◯) on each ten-frame to match the numeral on the truck.

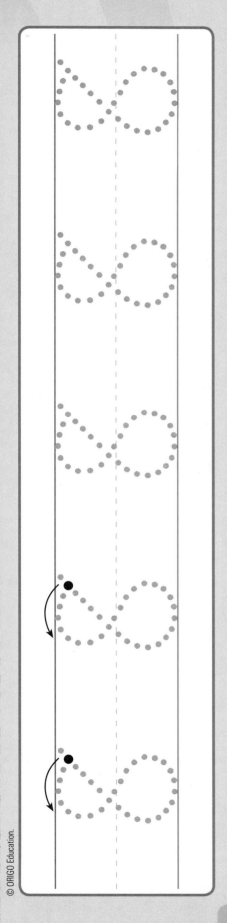
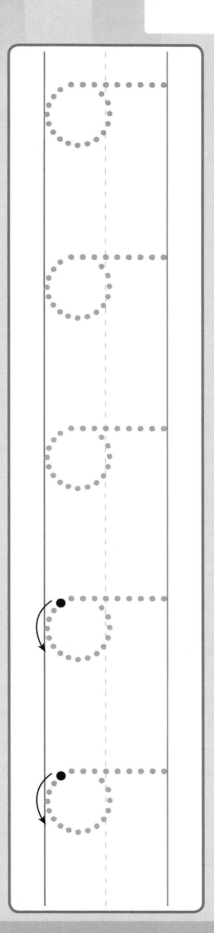
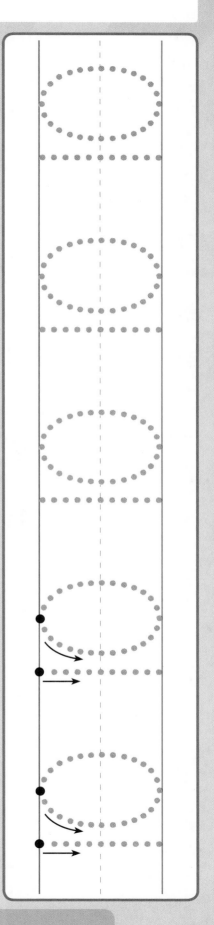

Have the student read the first numeral then trace it five times.
Repeat for the other numerals.

48

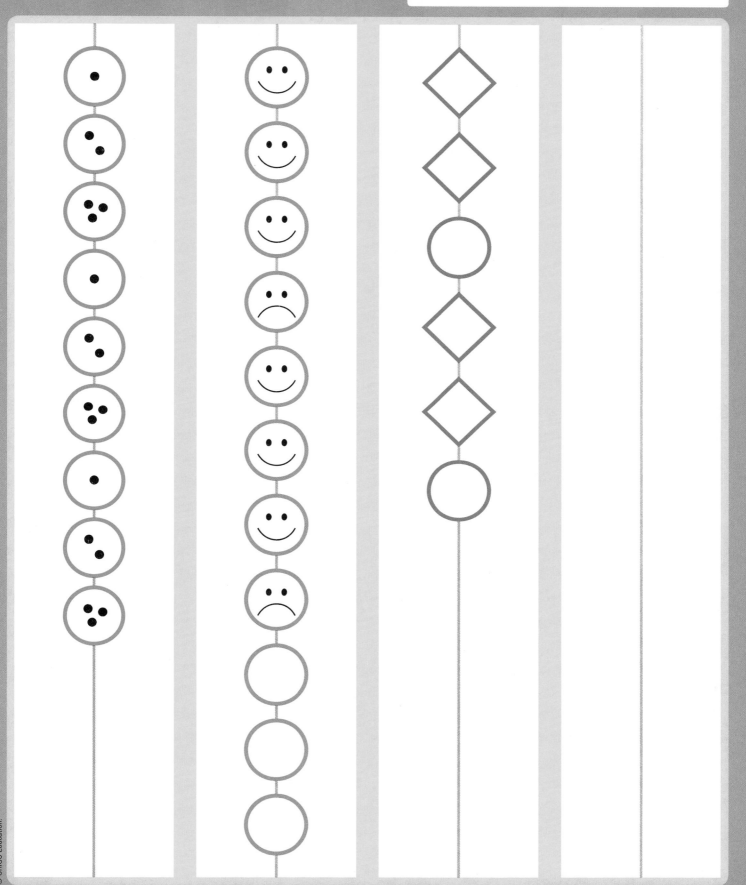

Have the student draw pictures to continue each repeating pattern, then draw their own repeating pattern on the last string.

a.

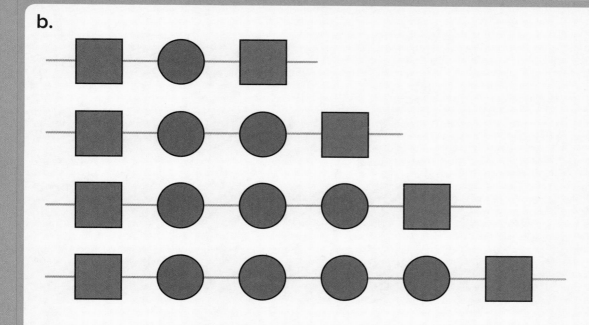

b.

Have the student describe each pattern then draw the next part of each pattern.

50

© ORIGO Education.

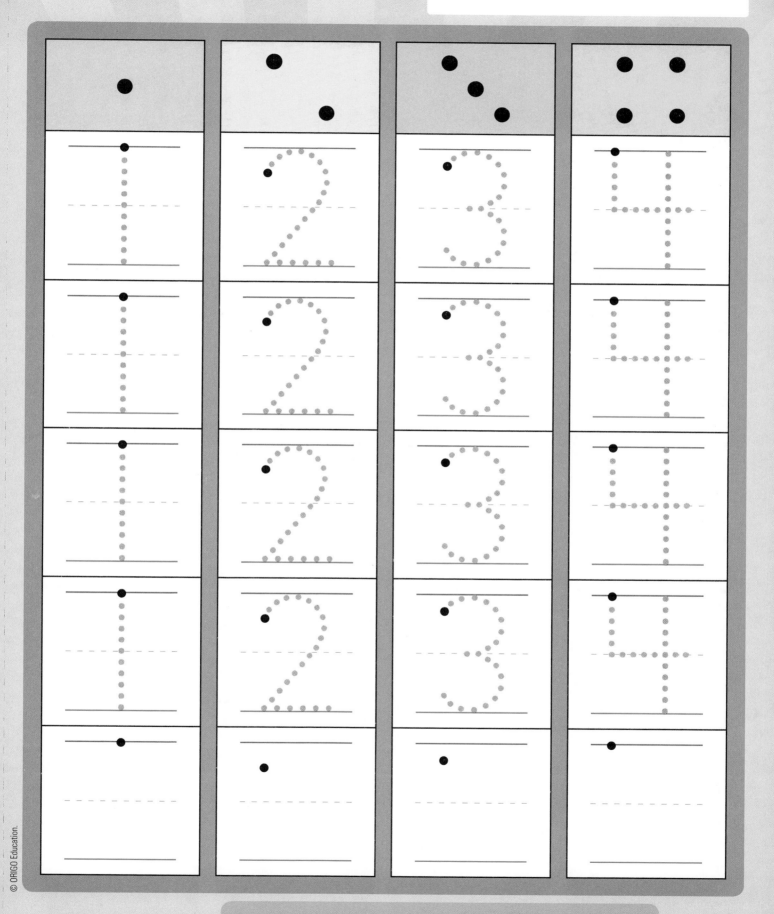

ORIGO Stepping Stones K • 6.6b

Have the student count the dots and read the matching number aloud, then write the numeral to complete the strip. Repeat for each strip.

51

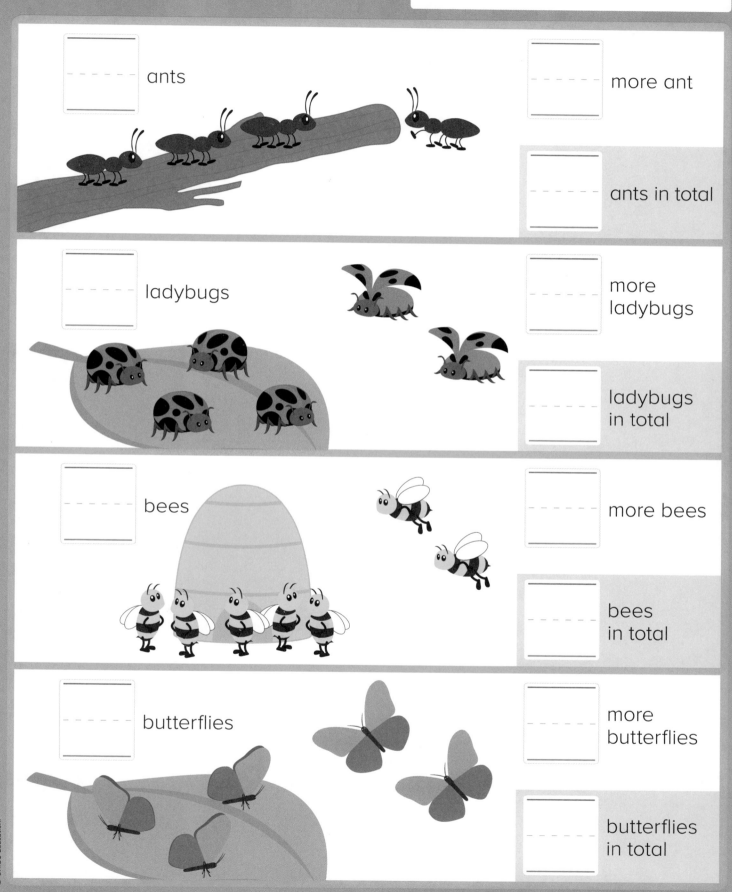

ants

more ant

ants in total

ladybugs

more
ladybugs

ladybugs
in total

bees

more bees

bees
in total

butterflies

more
butterflies

butterflies
in total

For each picture, have the student write the number in each group,
then write the total.

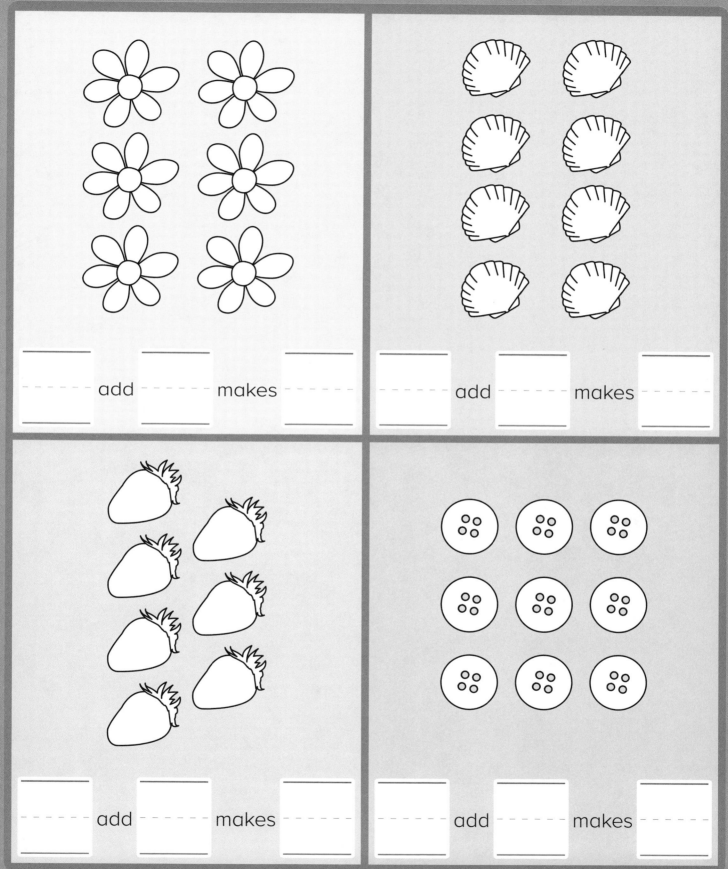

add ____ makes ____

add ____ makes ____

add ____ makes ____

add ____ makes ____

For each picture, have the student use two colors to show two different groups, then write the number in each group and the total.

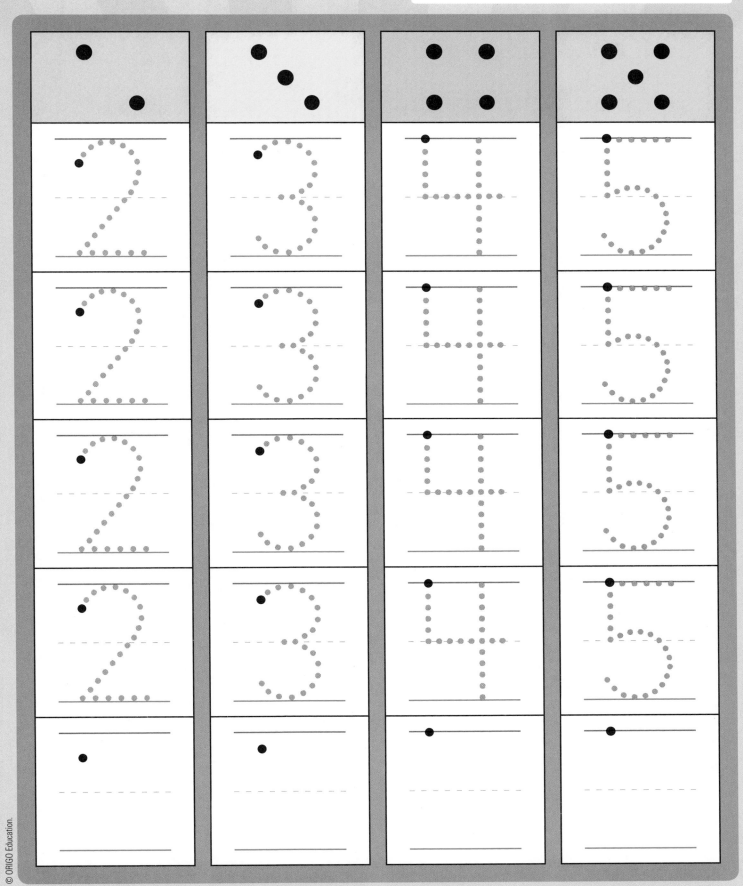

Have the student count the dots and read the matching number aloud, then write the numeral to complete the strip. Repeat for each strip.

a.

5 add 2 makes [ ]

b.

[ ] add [ ] makes [ ]

c.

[ ] add [ ] makes [ ]

d.

[ ] add [ ] makes [ ]

For each of these, have the student draw more faces to fill the frame, then write numerals to show the two groups and the total.

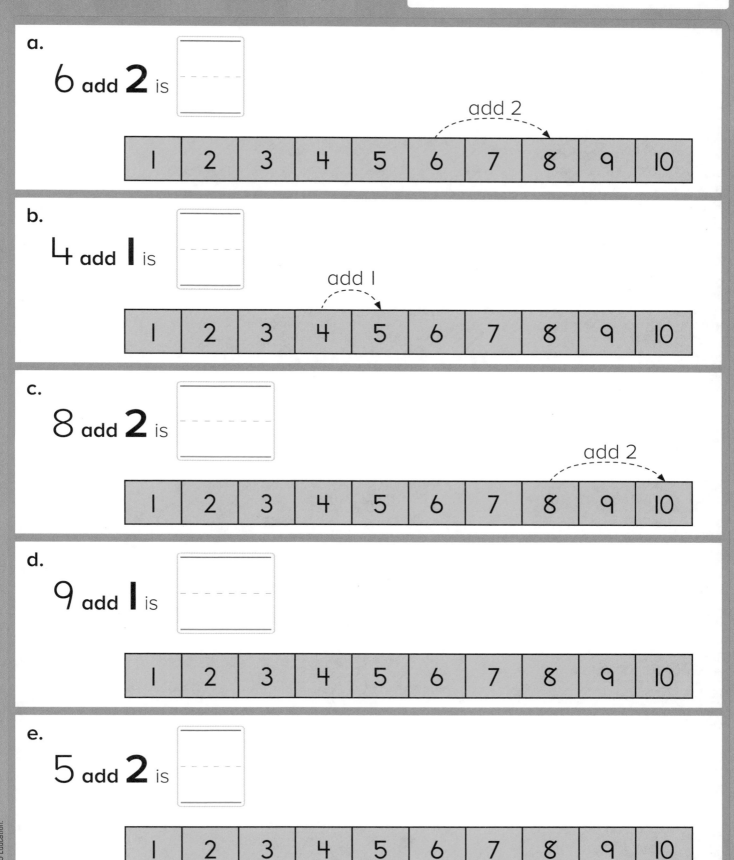

a. 6 add 2 is [ ]

1 2 3 4 5 6 7 8 9 10

add 2

b. 4 add 1 is [ ]

1 2 3 4 5 6 7 8 9 10

add 1

c. 8 add 2 is [ ]

1 2 3 4 5 6 7 8 9 10

add 2

d. 9 add 1 is [ ]

1 2 3 4 5 6 7 8 9 10

e. 5 add 2 is [ ]

1 2 3 4 5 6 7 8 9 10

For each number track, have the student draw a jump to add 1 or 2, then write the total.

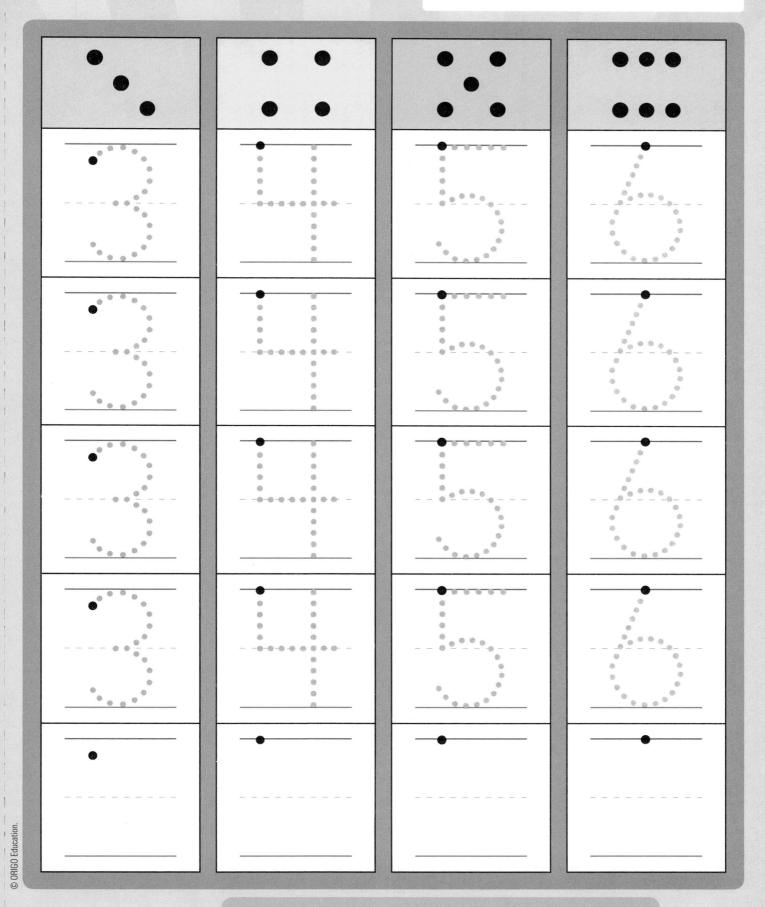

Have the student count the dots and read the matching number aloud,
then write the numeral to complete the strip. Repeat for each strip.

Lighter than a .

Heavier than a full .

Have the student draw objects that they know are lighter than a baseball and heavier than a full water bottle.

For each balance, have the student draw a line around the fruit that is heavier.

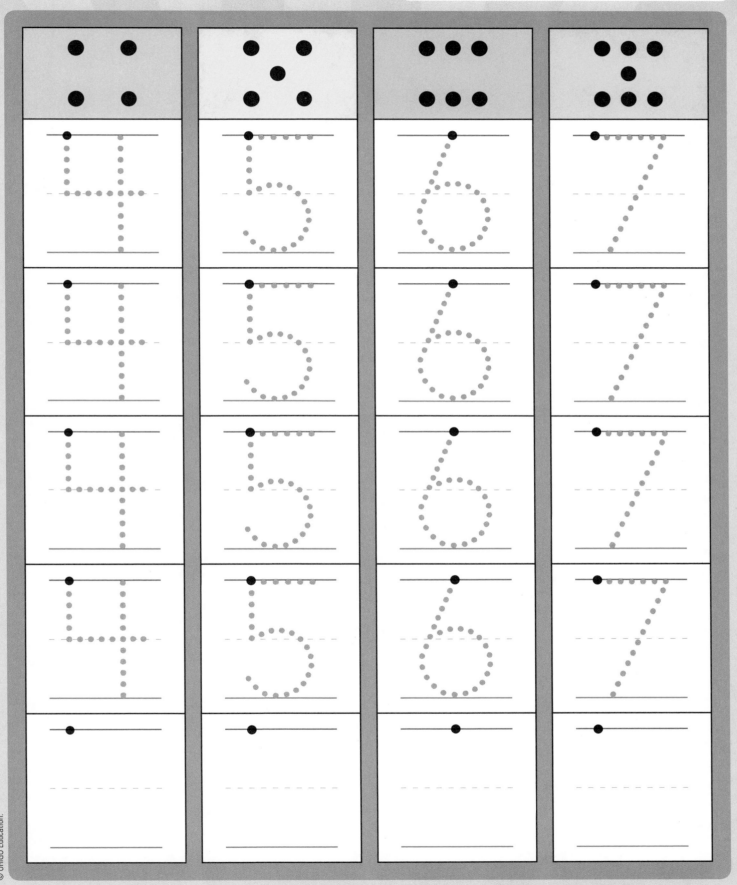

Have the student count the dots and read the matching number aloud, then write the numeral to complete the strip. Repeat for each strip.

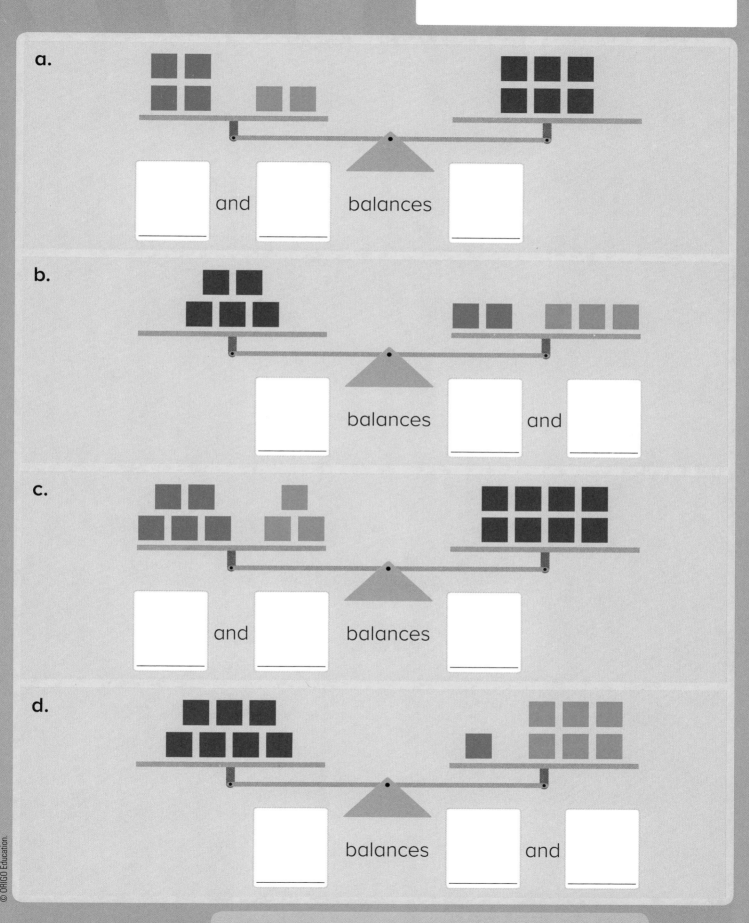

a.

[   ] and [   ]   balances   [   ]

b.

[   ]   balances   [   ] and [   ]

c.

[   ] and [   ]   balances   [   ]

d.

[   ]   balances   [   ] and [   ]

Have the student write numerals to match the two groups on one side, then write the total that balances the groups. Repeat for each balance picture.

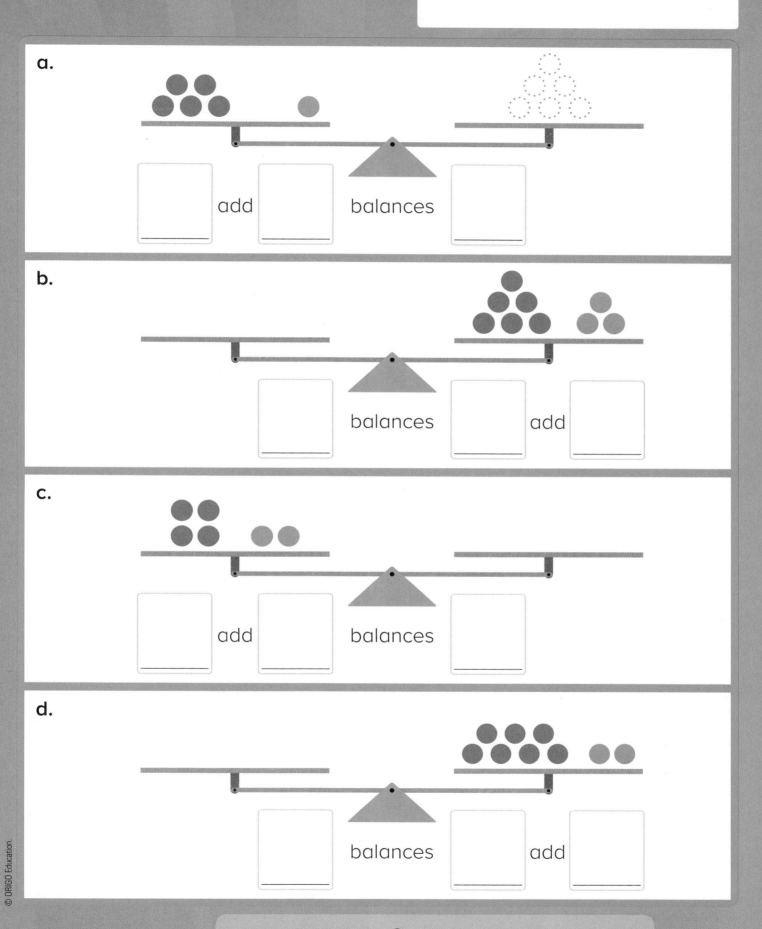

a.

☐ add ☐ balances ☐

b.

☐ balances ☐ add ☐

c.

☐ add ☐ balances ☐

d.

☐ balances ☐ add ☐

Have the student draw counters (○) to make the balance picture true, then write numerals to complete an addition sentence that matches. Repeat for all.

62

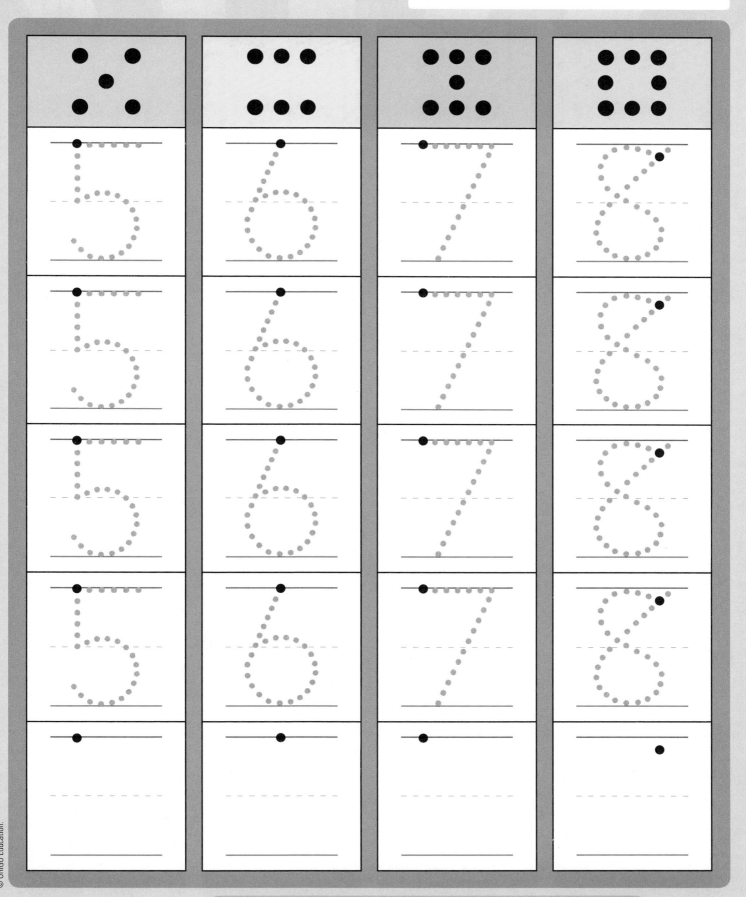

Have the student count the dots and read the matching number aloud,
then write the numeral to complete the strip. Repeat for each strip.

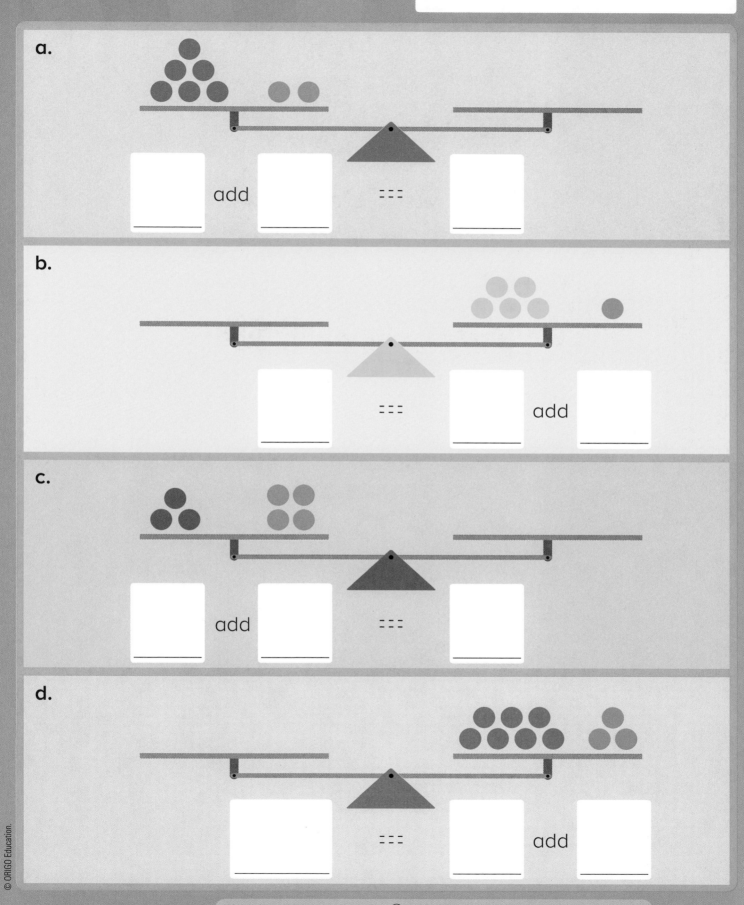

a. add ===

b. === add

c. add ===

d. === add

Have the student draw counters (◯) to make the balance picture true. Then write numerals and trace over the equals symbol to complete an addition sentence. Repeat for all.

64

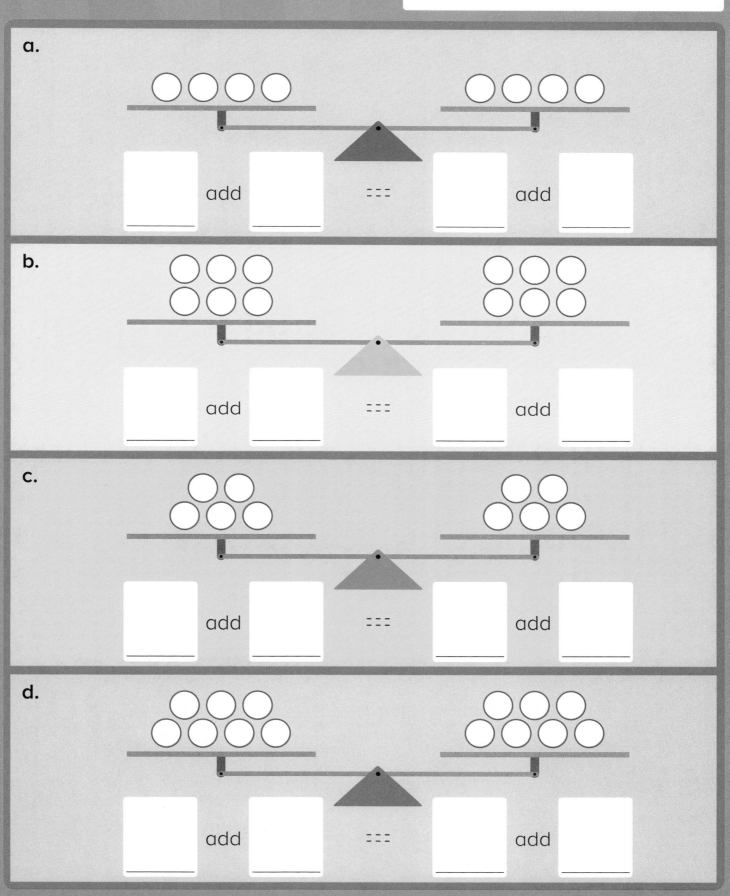

Have the student color **some** counters on each side of the balance, then write numerals and trace over the equals symbol to complete the addition sentence. Repeat for all.

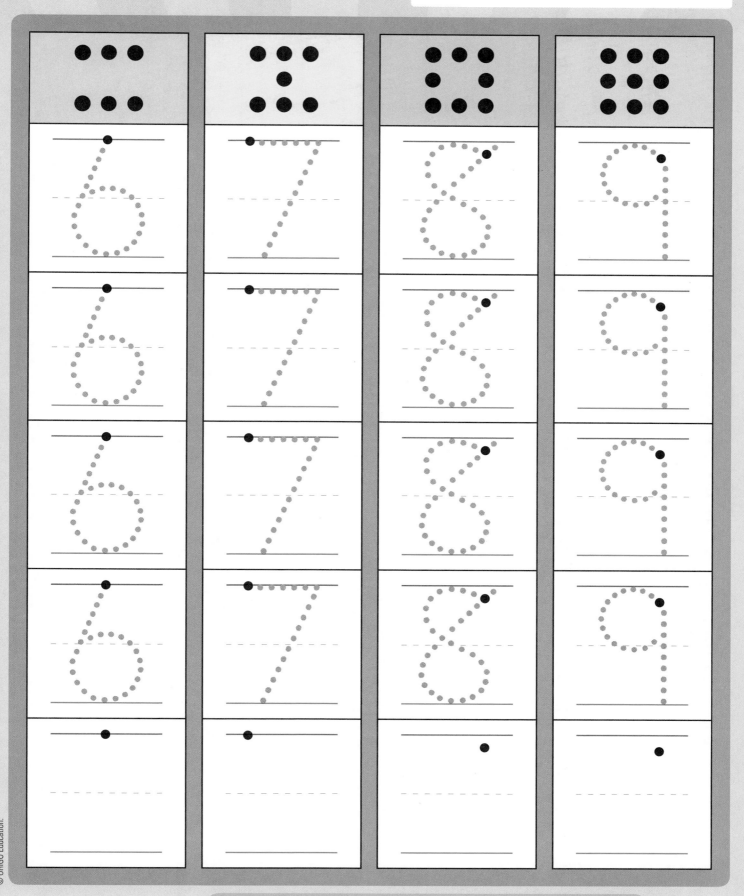

Have the student count the dots and read the matching number aloud, then write the numeral to complete the strip. Repeat for each strip.

all flat surfaces

all curved surfaces

flat and curved surfaces

Have the student draw or cut out one or two pictures of objects
from catalogs and paste them in a matching space above.

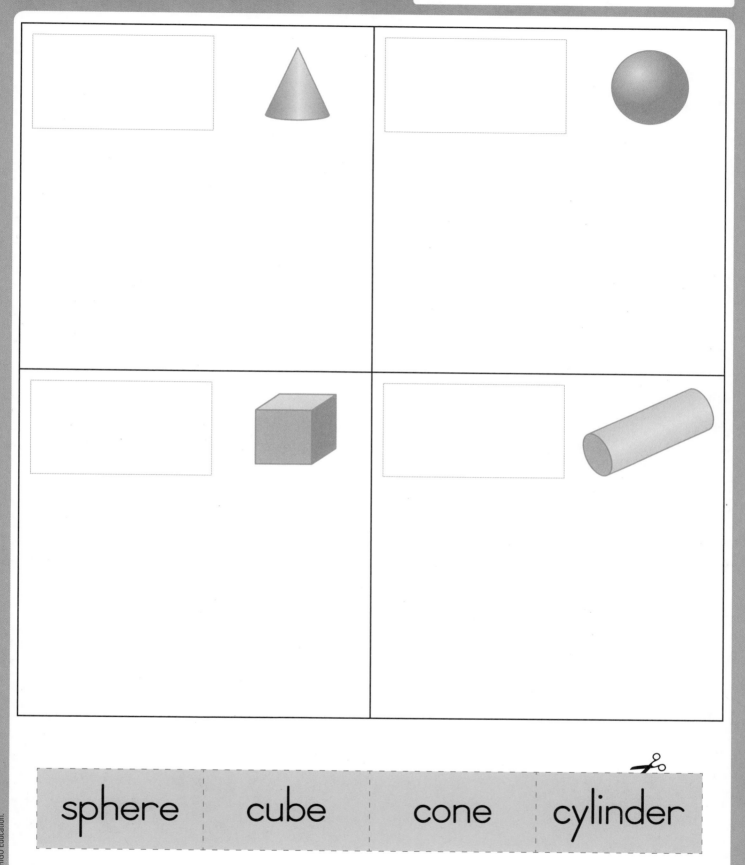

sphere | cube | cone | cylinder

Have the student cut out and paste each label beside a matching picture.
Then cut out one picture of a matching object from a catalog and
paste it in each remaining space.

68

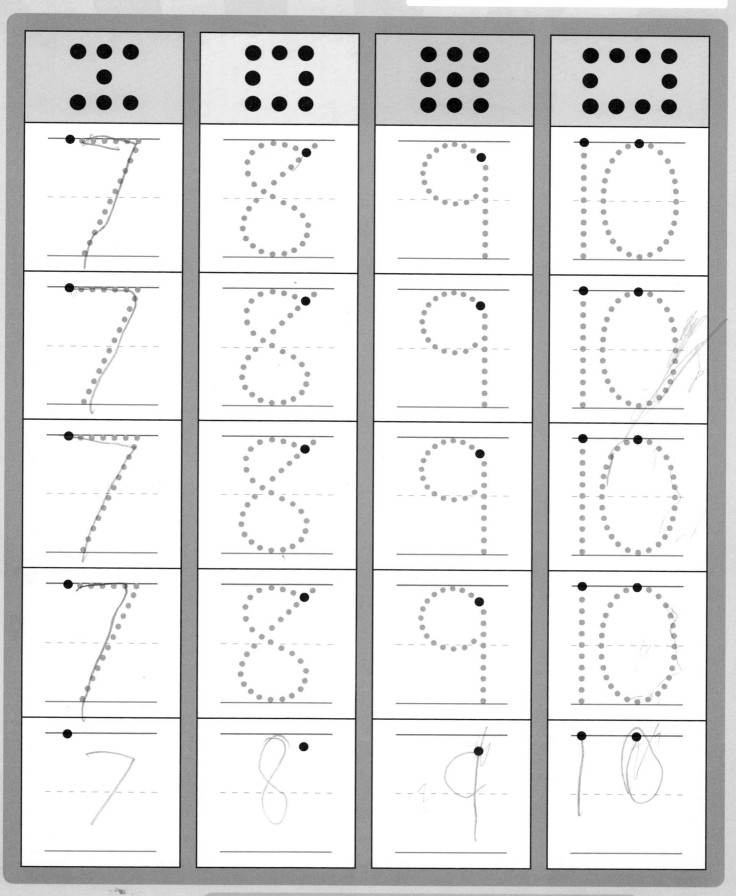

Have the student count the dots and read the matching number aloud, then write the numeral to complete the strip. Repeat for each strip.

a. Color 3 red.

[ ] + [ ] = [ ]

b. Color 5 red.

[ ] + [ ] = [ ]

c. Color 2 red.

[ ] + [ ] = [ ]

d. Color 6 red.

[ ] + [ ] = [ ]

Have the student color the number requested, then write a matching addition sentence.

a.

| 1 | + | 6 | = | |

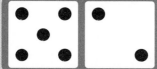

| 6 | + | 1 | = | |

b.

| | + | | = | |

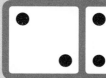

| | + | | = | |

c.

| | + | | = | |

| | + | | = | |

d.

| | + | | = | |

| | + | | = | |

e.

| | + | | = | |

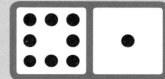

| | + | | = | |

f.

| | + | | = | |

| | + | | = | |

Have the student write two addition sentences to match the picture they see.

$8 + 2 =$ ___

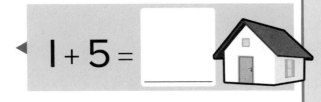

$1 + 5 =$ ___

$2 + 4 =$ ___

$2 + 2 =$ ___

$7 + 1 =$ ___

$9 + 1 =$ ___

$3 + 1 =$ ___

$2 + 6 =$ ___

$1 + 6 =$ ___

$1 + 4 =$ ___

$2 + 3 =$ ___

$5 + 2 =$ ___

ORIGO Stepping Stones **K** • 9.2b

Have the student write all the answers, then draw a line from each bunch of flowers to a house with a matching answer.

a.

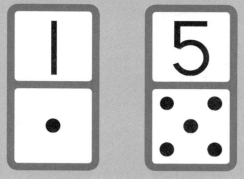

☐ + ☐ = ☐

b.

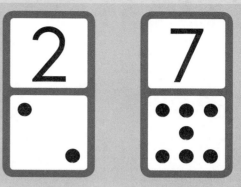

☐ + ☐ = ☐

c.

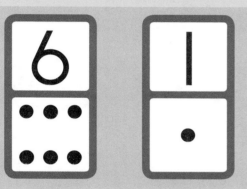

☐ + ☐ = ☐

d.

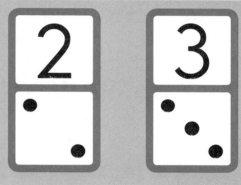

☐ + ☐ = ☐

e.

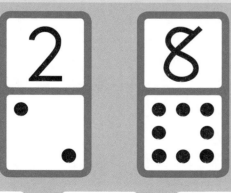

☐ + ☐ = ☐

f.

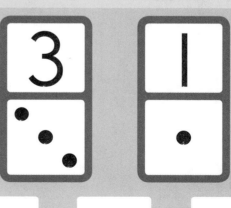

☐ + ☐ = ☐

Have the student say the greater number then count on to figure out the total.
Then ask the student to write the addition sentence with the greater number first.

a.

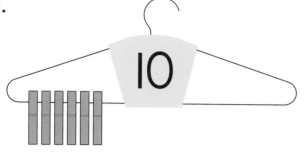

6 + ☐ = ☐

b.

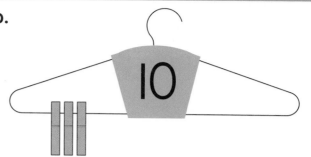

☐ = ☐ + ☐

c.

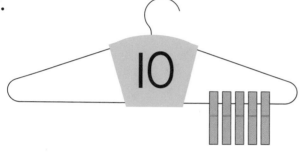

☐ + ☐ = ☐

d.

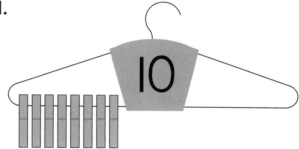

☐ = ☐ + ☐

e.

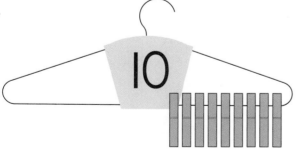

☐ + ☐ = ☐

f.

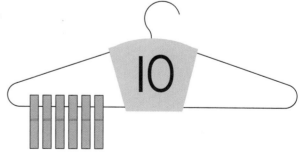

☐ = ☐ + ☐

Have the student draw more clothespins to make a total of 10, then write a matching addition sentence.

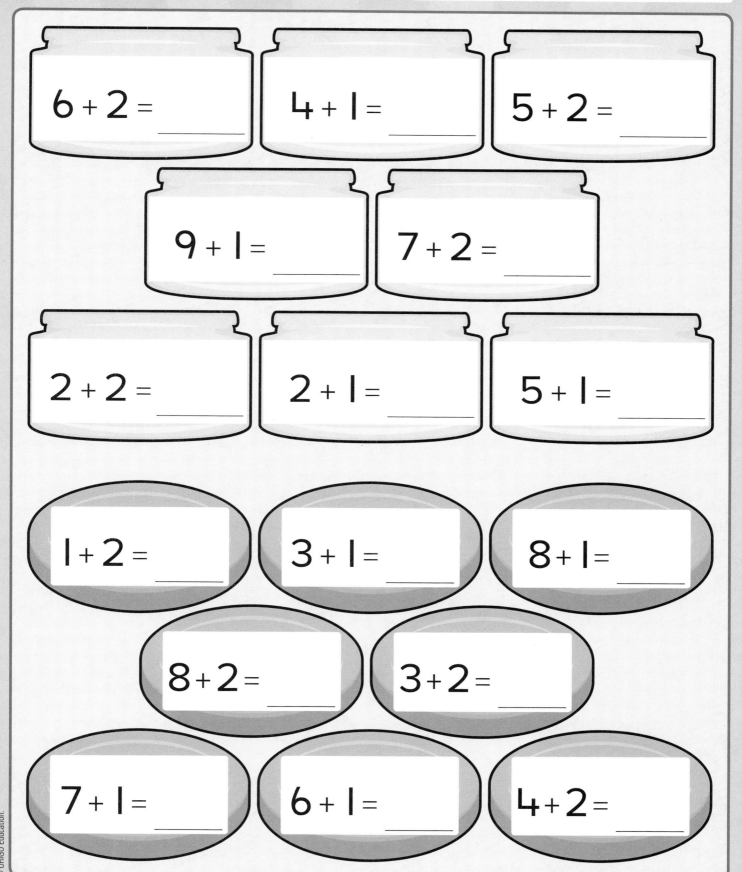

6 + 2 = _____

4 + 1 = _____

5 + 2 = _____

9 + 1 = _____

7 + 2 = _____

2 + 2 = _____

2 + 1 = _____

5 + 1 = _____

1 + 2 = _____

3 + 1 = _____

8 + 1 = _____

8 + 2 = _____

3 + 2 = _____

7 + 1 = _____

6 + 1 = _____

4 + 2 = _____

ORIGO Stepping Stones K • 9.4b

Have the student write all the answers, then find jars and lids with the same answer and color their labels the same.

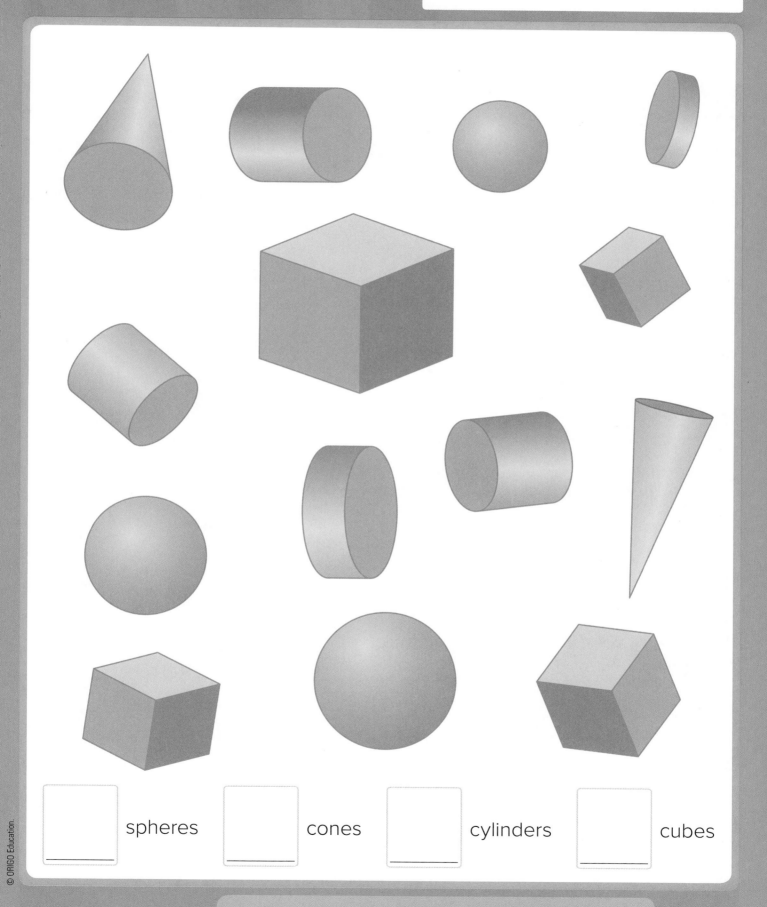

	spheres		cones		cylinders		cubes

Have the student cross out all the spheres then write the total in the box.
Ask the student to use a different color and repeat for each of the other objects.

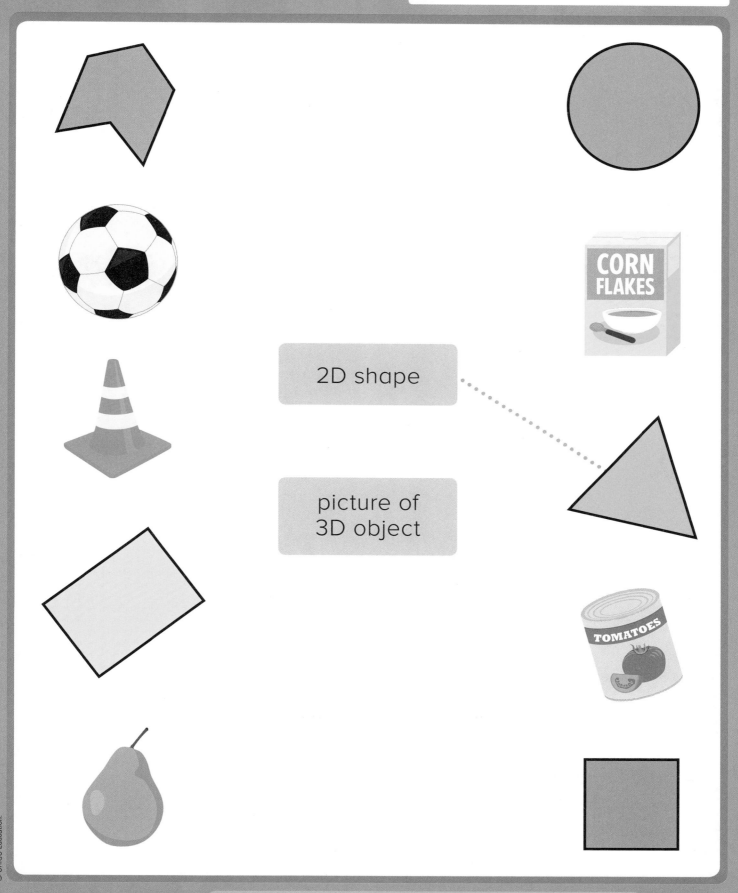

2D shape

picture of 3D object

Have the student look at each picture and decide if it is a 2D shape or a picture of a 3D object, then draw a line to the label to show their decision. Encourage the student to justify their decision.

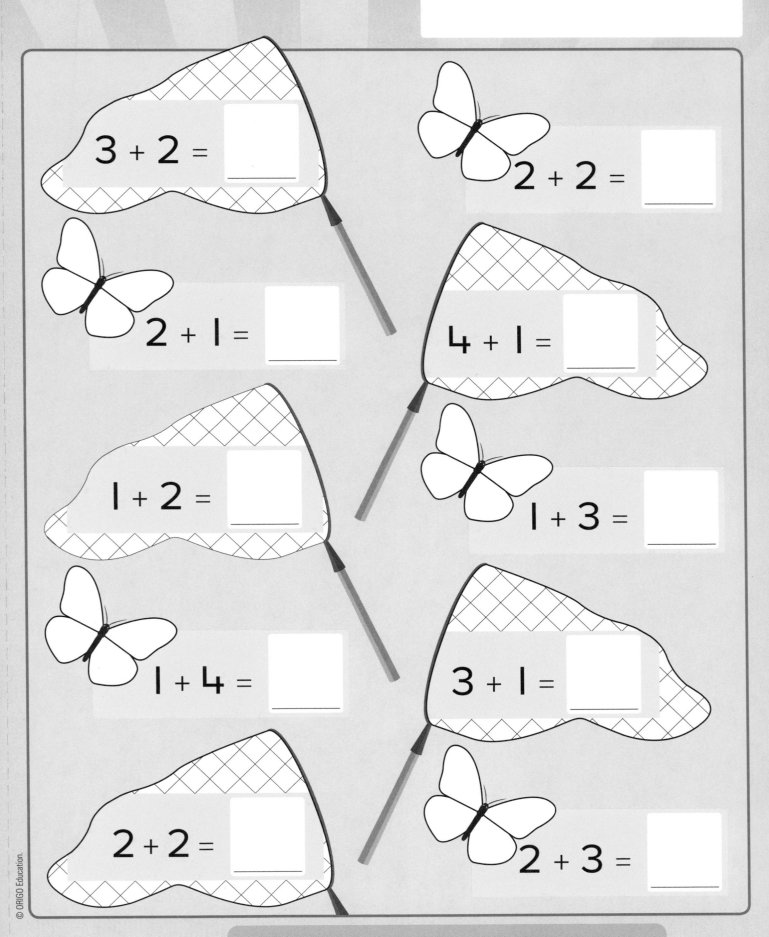

$3 + 2 =$ ____

$2 + 2 =$ ____

$2 + 1 =$ ____

$4 + 1 =$ ____

$1 + 2 =$ ____

$1 + 3 =$ ____

$1 + 4 =$ ____

$3 + 1 =$ ____

$2 + 2 =$ ____

$2 + 3 =$ ____

Have the students write all the answers then color each addition sentence and its turnaround the same.

_____ ants in total

_____ bugs in total

_____ walk away

_____ hop away

_____ ducks in total

_____ ladybugs in total

_____ walks away

_____ fly away

For each of these, have the student count the total number and write the numeral, then write the number going away.

Show 6 pennies. You spend 4.

1¢   1¢

1¢   1¢

1¢   1¢

Show 9 nuts. You eat 5.

Show 5 eggs. You break 2.

Show 7 marbles. You take 3.

For each of these, have the student draw pictures to show the total, then cross out the number shown.

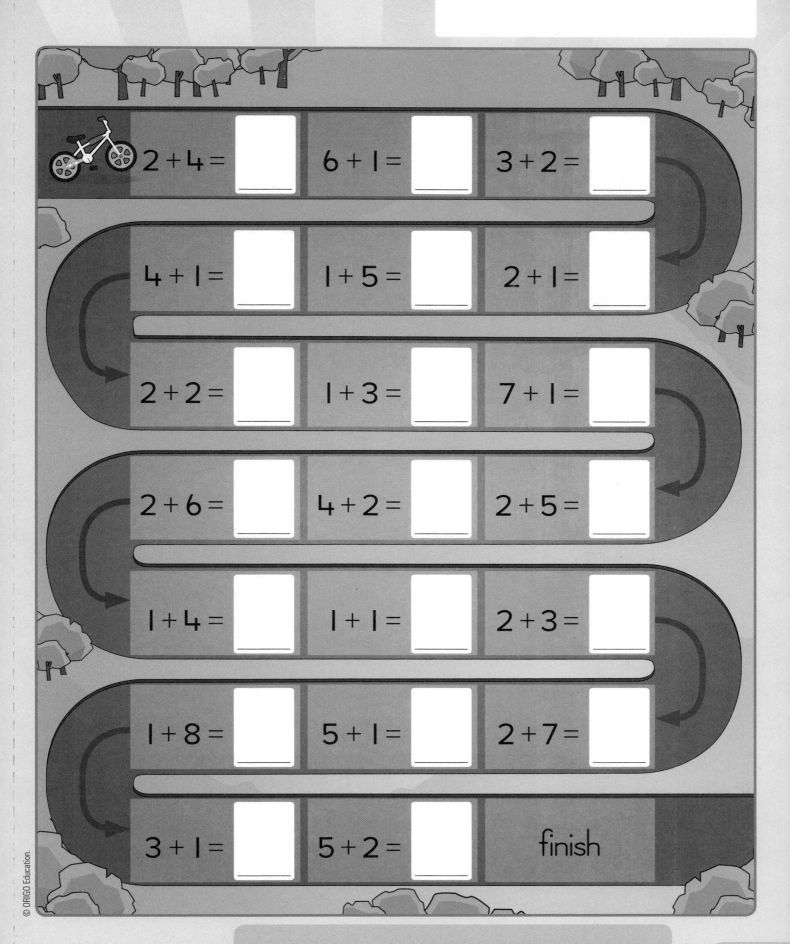

2 + 4 =

6 + 1 =

3 + 2 =

4 + 1 =

1 + 5 =

2 + 1 =

2 + 2 =

1 + 3 =

7 + 1 =

2 + 6 =

4 + 2 =

2 + 5 =

1 + 4 =

1 + 1 =

2 + 3 =

1 + 8 =

5 + 1 =

2 + 7 =

3 + 1 =

5 + 2 =

finish

Have the student figure out each answer quickly and write it on the track.

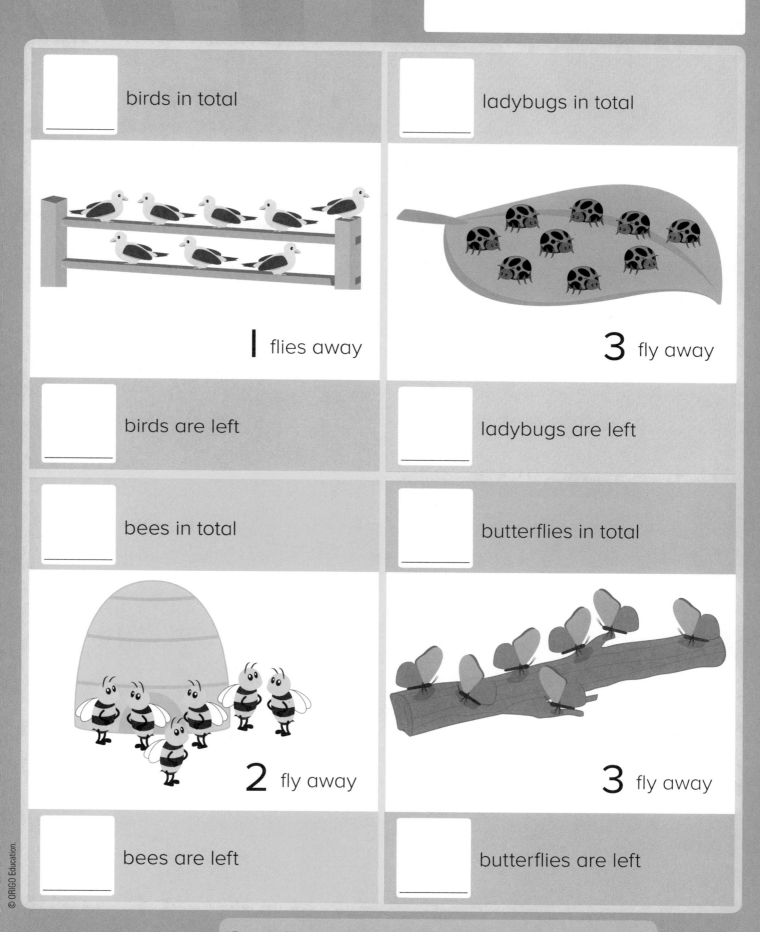

___ birds in total

I flies away

___ birds are left

___ bees in total

2 fly away

___ bees are left

___ ladybugs in total

3 fly away

___ ladybugs are left

___ butterflies in total

3 fly away

___ butterflies are left

For each of these, have the student write the total number, cross some out to match the story, then write the number left.

a.

 cover **2** = ⬜

b.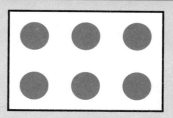

⬜ cover **1** = ⬜

c.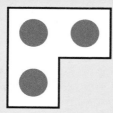

⬜ cover **1** = ⬜

d.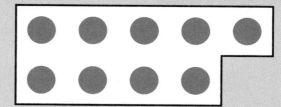

⬜ cover **2** = ⬜

e.

⬜ cover **2** = ⬜

f.

⬜ cover **1** = ⬜

g.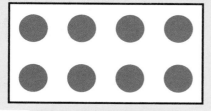

⬜ cover **1** = ⬜

h.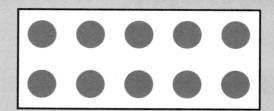

⬜ cover **2** = ⬜

Have the student write the total number of dots, then cover the dots (as shown in "a") and write the number of dots they can see.

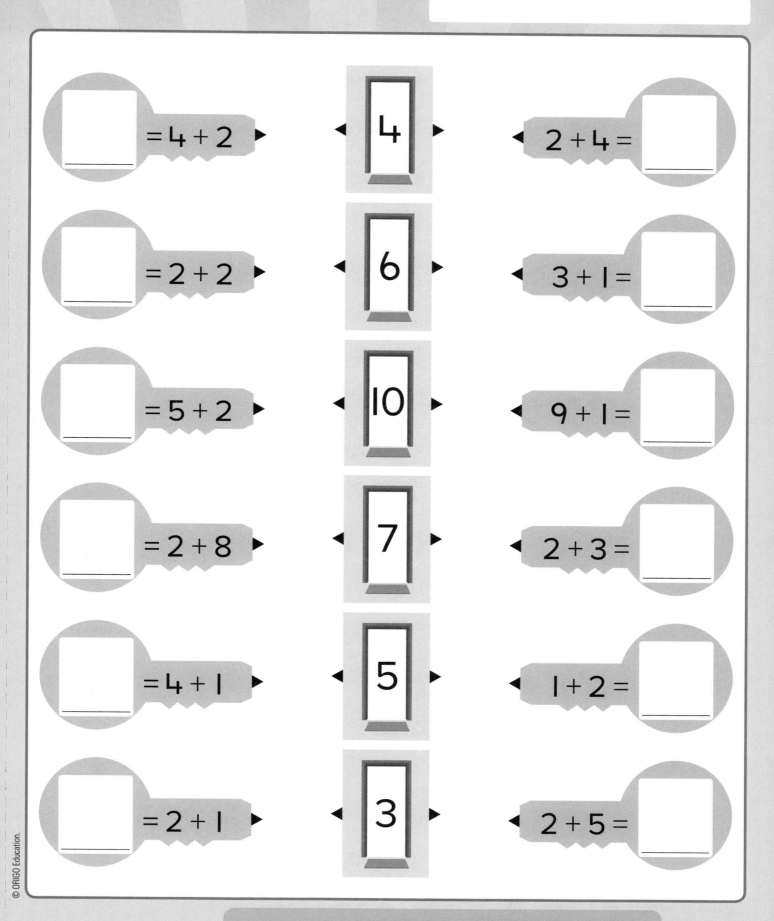

Have the student figure out and write the answers, then draw a line
from each key to a matching door. There are two keys for each door.

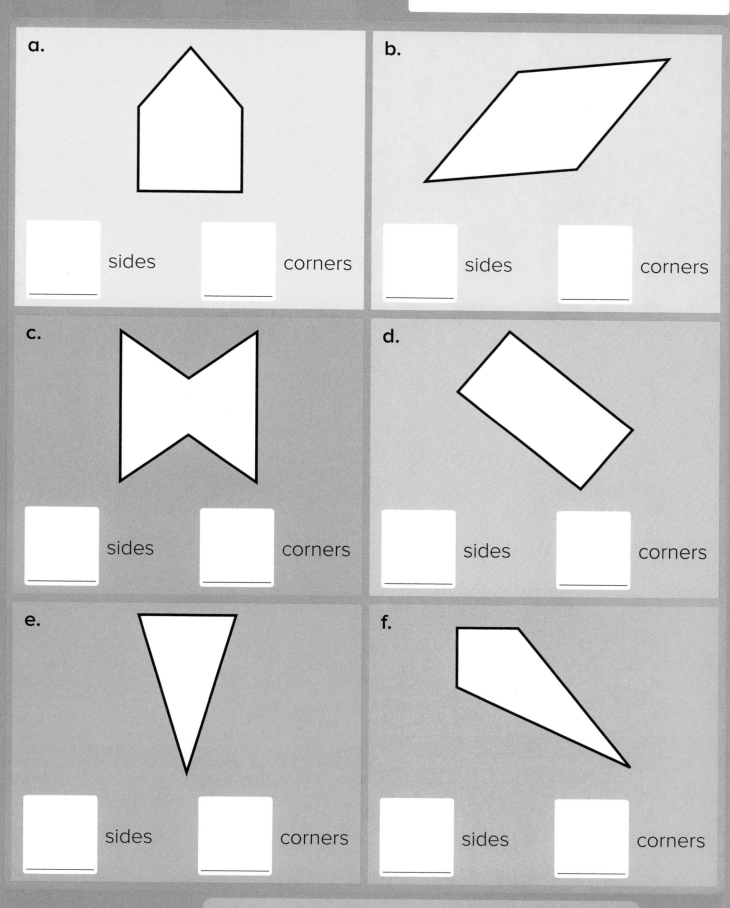

a.

☐ sides   ☐ corners

b.

☐ sides   ☐ corners

c.

☐ sides   ☐ corners

d.

☐ sides   ☐ corners

e.

☐ sides   ☐ corners

f.

☐ sides   ☐ corners

Have the student count and write the number of sides and corners on each shape.

85

circles	triangles

square rectangles	non-square rectangles

Have the student cut out the 2D shapes, then sort and paste them in the correct box.

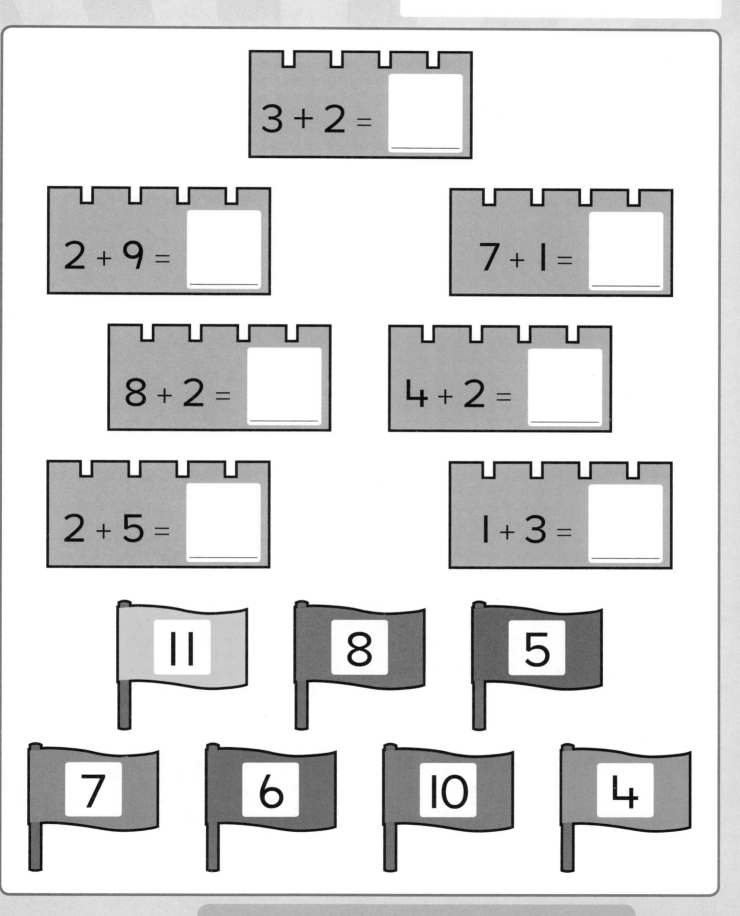

3 + 2 =

2 + 9 =

7 + 1 =

8 + 2 =

4 + 2 =

2 + 5 =

1 + 3 =

11   8   5

7   6   10   4

Have the student write each answer then draw a line from each castle to its matching flag.

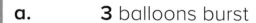

a. **3** balloons burst

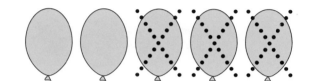

5 − 3 =

b. **2** balloons burst

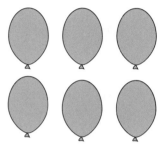

− =

c. **4** balloons burst

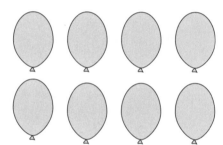

− =

d. **6** balloons burst

− =

e. **5** balloons burst

− =

f. **2** balloons burst

− =

Have the student cross out the number of balloons that burst then complete the subtraction sentence.

88

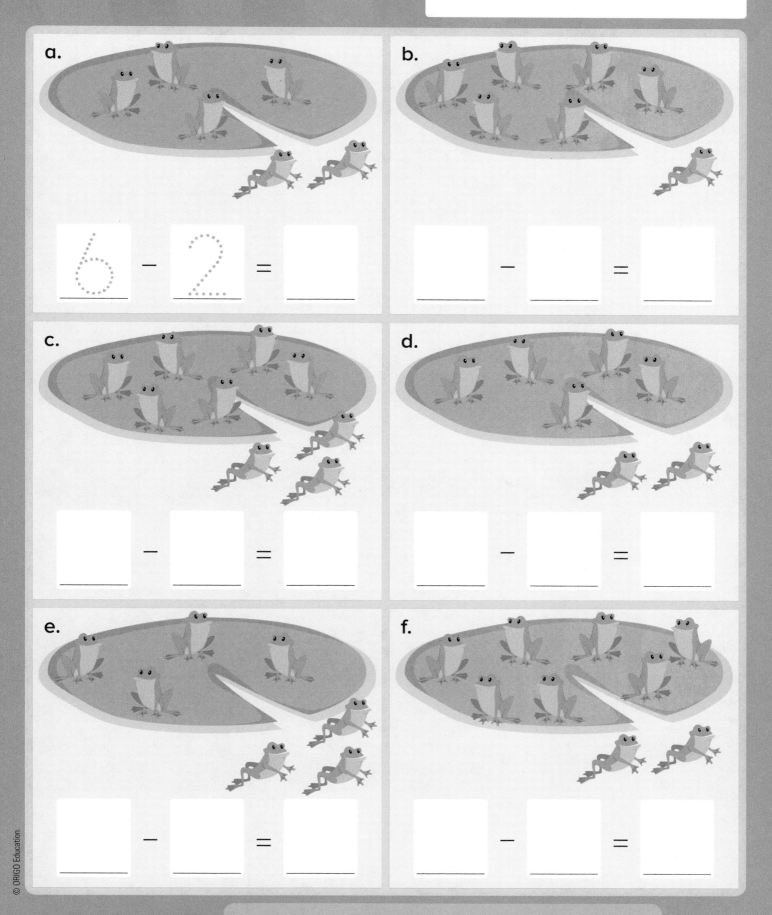

a. $6 - 2 =$

b. $\_\_ - \_\_ = \_\_$

c. $\_\_ - \_\_ = \_\_$

d. $\_\_ - \_\_ = \_\_$

e. $\_\_ - \_\_ = \_\_$

f. $\_\_ - \_\_ = \_\_$

Have the student write the total number of frogs and the number jumping away, then complete the subtraction sentence.

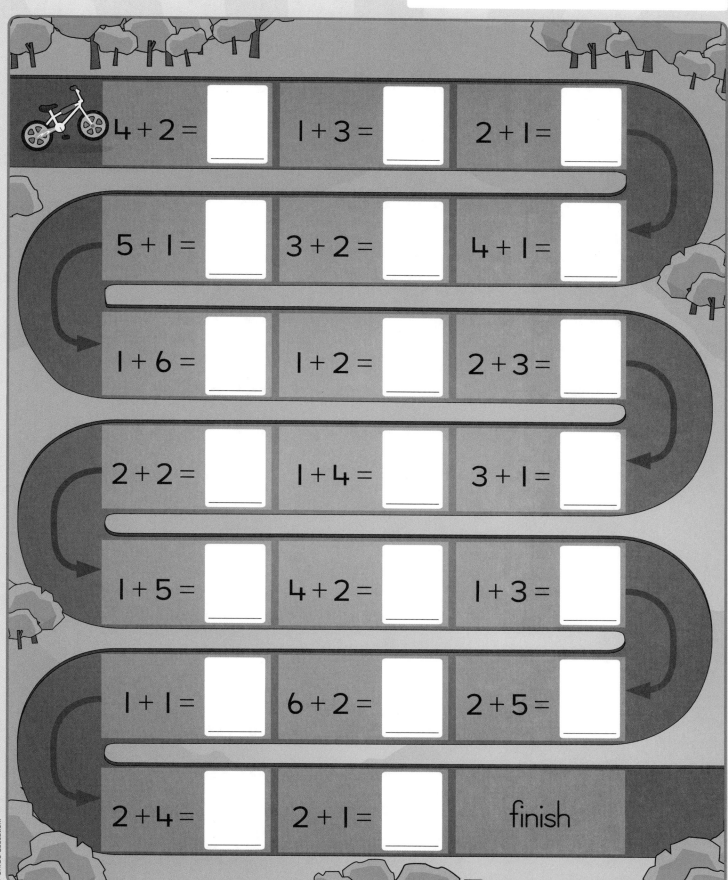

4 + 2 =

1 + 3 =

2 + 1 =

5 + 1 =

3 + 2 =

4 + 1 =

1 + 6 =

1 + 2 =

2 + 3 =

2 + 2 =

1 + 4 =

3 + 1 =

1 + 5 =

4 + 2 =

1 + 3 =

1 + 1 =

6 + 2 =

2 + 5 =

2 + 4 =

2 + 1 =

finish

Have the student figure out each answer quickly and write it on the track.

17 seventeen

16 sixteen

14 fourteen

Have the student place 17 pennies (or any small item) in the empty space, then trace over the matching number name. Ask the student to remove all the pennies, then repeat for 16 and 14.

15	fifteen
19	nineteen
18	eighteen

Have the student place 15 pennies (or any small item) in the empty space, then trace over the matching number name. Ask the student to remove all the pennies, then repeat for 19 and 18.

$7 + 2 =$

$2 + 5 =$

$7 + 1 =$

$8 + 1 =$

$1 + 6 =$

$2 + 2 =$

$5 + 1 =$

$6 + 2 =$

$3 + 1 =$

$4 + 2 =$

Have the student figure out and write the answer on each kite and tail, then draw lines to join kites and tails that have the same answer.

a.

b.

c.

Have the student copy each picture. Ask the student to say all the shape names they know.

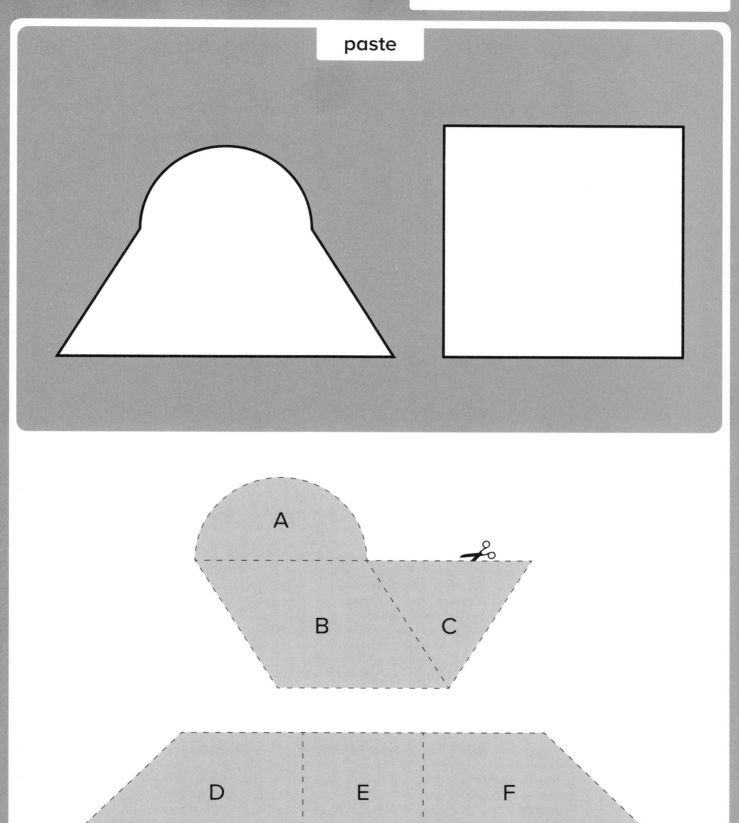

Have the student cut along all the dotted lines to make six shapes,
then paste the shapes to match each outline.

95

$2 + 5 =$ ____

$2 + 1 =$ ____

$5 + 1 =$ ____

$2 + 2 =$ ____

$3 + 2 =$ ____

$8 + 2 =$ ____

$1 + 1 =$ ____

$1 + 7 =$ ____

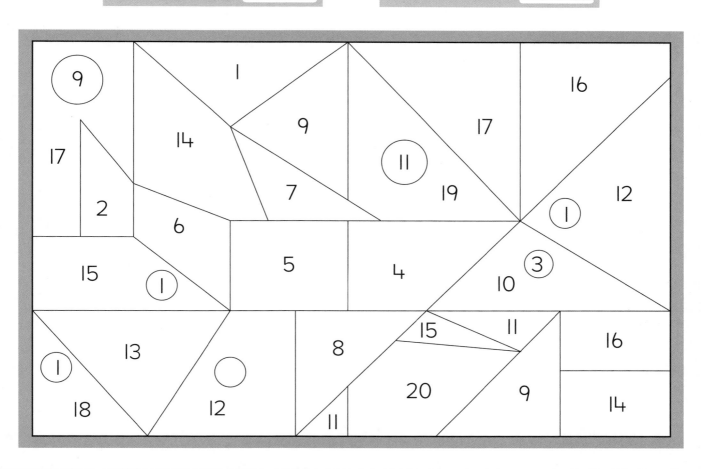

Have the student write the answers then find each answer in the puzzle
and color that part gray, then color the other parts blue.

Have the student place 11 pennies (or any small item) in the empty space, then trace over the matching number name. Ask the student to remove all the pennies, then repeat for 13 and 12.

a.

ten and [ ] **more**

b.

ten and [ ] **more**

c.

ten and [ ] **more**

d.

ten and [ ] **more**

For each, have the student draw a line around ten of the shapes,
then count how many **more** and write the number.

4 − 2 =

3 + 1 =

5 − 1 =

5 − 4 =

2 + 2 =

4 − 3 =

2 + 1 =

1 + 1 =

3 + 2 =

3 − 1 =

5 − 2 =

2 − 1 =

2 + 3 =

1 + 2 =

5 − 3 =

4 − 3 =

5 − 4 =

2 + 1 =

5 − 2 =

3 − 1 =

finish

ORIGO Stepping Stones K • 12.2b

Have the student figure out each answer quickly and write it on the track.

99

a.

_____ ten and _____ ones

b.

_____ ten and _____ ones

c.

_____ ten and _____ ones

d.

_____ ten and _____ ones

e.

_____ ten and _____ ones

Have the student write the number of tens and ones.

100

12	17	19
15	11	20
18	13	16
thirteen	sixteen	eleven
eighteen	twenty	seventeen
twelve	nineteen	fifteen

Have the student cut out all the pictures, then paste matching pictures together on a sheet of paper.

How does the sea say hello?

7 − 1 = 6

1 + 1 =

5 − 1 =

1 + 2 =

5 + 2 =

7 − 2 =

3 − 2 =

= 3 + 1

6 = 4 + 2

= 1 + 6

= 5 − 3

= 4 − 1

= 4 − 3

= 4 + 1

t i w s e v a

4 6 2 1 5 3 7

ORIGO Stepping Stones K • 12.4b

Read the question aloud. Explain that solving the puzzle will provide the answer. Have the student write the answers, draw straight lines to connect matching totals, and write the letters on each line above the matching answers at the bottom of the page.

102

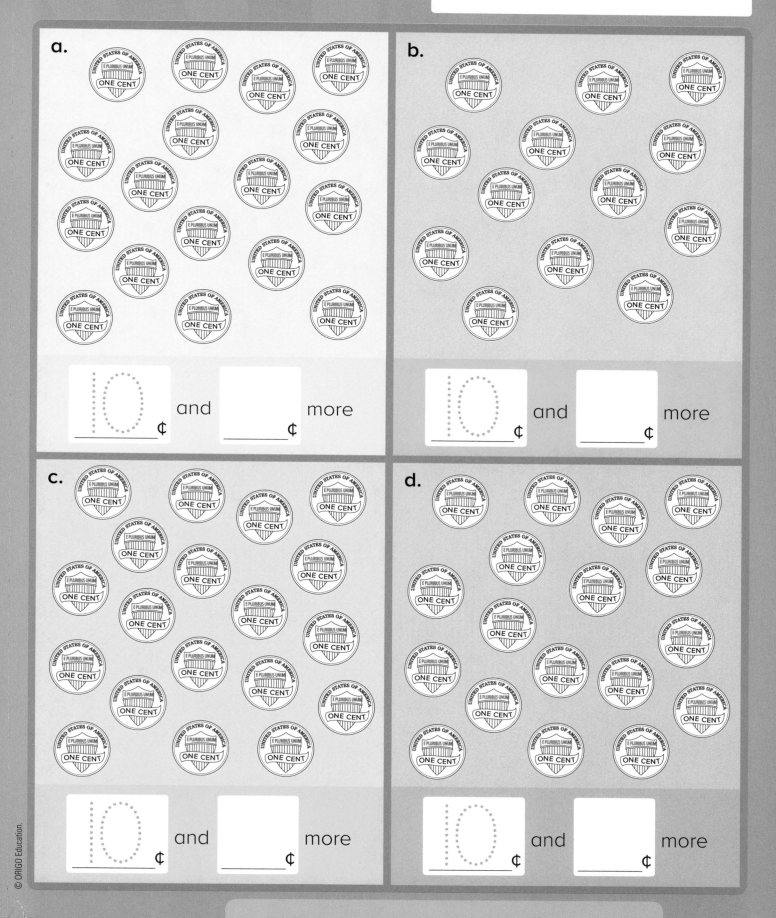

a. 10 and ____ more
____¢   ____¢

b. 10 and ____ more
____¢   ____¢

c. 10 and ____ more
____¢   ____¢

d. 10 and ____ more
____¢   ____¢

Have the student color ten pennies, then write the number of cents.

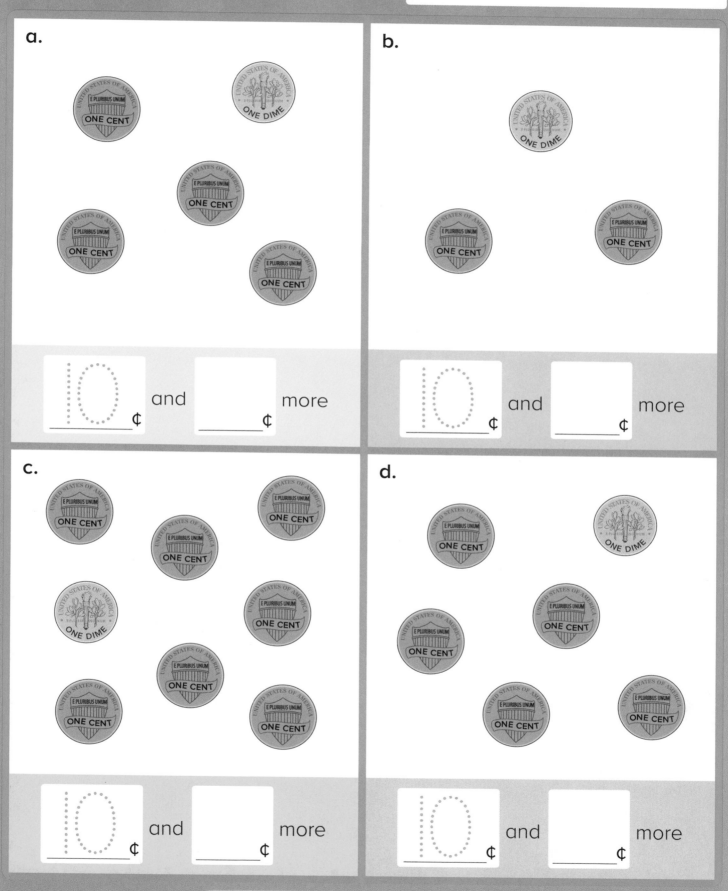

a.

10¢ and ___¢ more

b.

10¢ and ___¢ more

c.

10¢ and ___¢ more

d.

10¢ and ___¢ more

Have the student draw a line around the dime and count the number of pennies, then write the numbers.

How do you saw the sea in half?

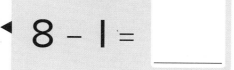

5 − 3 = 2

8 − 1 = ___

3 + 2 = ___

7 + 1 = ___

2 + 5 = ___

3 − 1 = 2

8 + 1 = ___

4 + 2 = ___

5 − 2 = ___

4 + 1 = ___

5 + 1 = ___

4 − 1 = ___

6 + 2 = ___

7 + 2 = ___

(i) (e) (h) (s) (t) (a) (w)

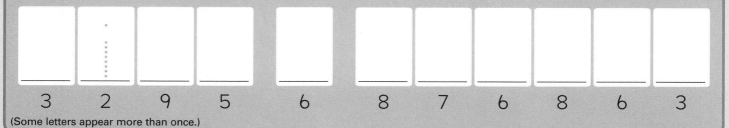

3	2	9	5	6	8	7	6	8	6	3

(Some letters appear more than once.)

© ORIGO Education.

Read the question aloud. Explain that solving the puzzle will provide the answer. Have the student write the answers, draw straight lines to connect matching totals, and write the letters on each line above the matching answers at the bottom of the page.

105